Also by Rosemary Miner:

ONCE UPON A TIME TO DIE FOR

The year is 1873 when on a late October night Grace Wickham is called to an accident at the local tannery. Recently returned from a year of medical school, Miss Wickham is the person people turn to as they once did her late father, the local doctor.

The body floating in a steaming tannery vat is the owner, Truman Reed, and the men who rush to answer the emergency bell each have reason to wish him dead. With the constable out of town, the coroner asks Gracie to look into things, for this was no accident.

Is the murderer the manager himself whom Reed threatened to fire? Was it his partner, Phineas Pierce, who wanted to sell? Troublemaker Wash Baker, whose pay had been cut? Recently fired night watchman Orrin Rooney? Reed's embittered wife? Or Chester Owens, who believes his son died following Reed's unreasonable orders? And why was a peddler hanging around the tannery that night?

As Gracie sees patients in her herbal practice and talks with neighbors, she puzzles over motives and evidence with Adirondack hotel owner and friend, Ambrose Baldoon, (the only man taller than Gracie's six feet). Another suspicious death complicates her investigation until clues converge and Gracie comes up with some surprising answers.

LIES & LOGS
TO DIE FOR

Rosemary Miner

Rosemary Miner

HILLIARD HARRIS

HILLIARD HARRIS

P.O. Box 275
Boonsboro, Maryland 21713-0275

Lies And Logs To Die For Copyright © 2008
by Rosemary Miner

First Edition-April 2008
ISBN 1-59133-255-9
978-1-59133-255-8

Book Design: S. A. Reilly
Cover Illustration © S. A. Reilly
Manufactured/Printed in the United States of America
2008

To Scott, Todd and Matthew

Acknowledgements:

While this is a work of fiction much of the descriptions of Adirondack logging camps and the river drive came from research at the Adirondack Museum and interviewing local people. I was fortunate to spend time with John Paradis who started in the woods as a youngster, gradually mastering all the skills a forester needed before Finch Pruyn Paper Corporation chose him to direct its operations in Glens Falls, New York. His knowledge of the industry is encyclopedic.

Two daughters of the late river superintendent John Donahue, Helen Donahue and Milda Donahue Burns, still live in North River and graciously told me about their father and how he engineered the Hudson River log drive. Milda gives talks to local historical societies and other groups on this subject, but to have her go over a map of ponds, lakes, and tributaries that pore into the rivers was a memorable history lesson in her home. Her enthusiasm and knowledge are gifts she shares with her listeners. I put into the words of some of my characters a few of the stories the sisters told. Again thanks to Milda for that wonderful childhood tale of innocently visiting "the cat house."

"Milly, M.D." by Helen Dann Stringer has the true incident for teasing a woman student in anatomy class in the 19th century. I fictionalized it for my character, Grace Wickham, as well as her time at Syracuse Medical College.

The last Hudson River drive ended in the 1950's when the logs that came down to the Glens Falls mills were for pulp. Today logs continue to travel down to Glens Falls on the back of huge trucks on the Northway's Interstate 87.

I once more thank first born and first reader Scott Miner, Todd Miner, and recently their brother, Matthew, who finished the manuscript by lantern light when we lost power.

An early draft was critiqued by Sisters in Crime which was helpful. I thank Bob Foley, Helen Wagar, Bonnie Vicki, Sue Ocsher, Becky Milner and other members of the North Country Writers for reading various pages and making suggestions. I am especially grateful to retired M.D. Wes Dingman for his careful reading of all the chapters and answering my medical questions. Linda Bassarab is the computer whiz who corrects my mistakes and offers suggestions. The writer Bibi Wein taught workshops for the Adirondack Center for Writing where many of these pages were critiqued and has become a good friend who invariably pushes me to do better. I thank them all.

One

Grace Wickham entered the train carrying a small valise as she searched for an empty seat. Her above average height and fiery orange hair turned heads as she strode down the aisle of the passenger car in a flowing black cape and wide brimmed hat. Both her stature and striking hair came from her late father. She wore the black hat to cover what she could of the despised hair color. But at six-foot there was little she could do to mask her height.

Gracie was on her way home from the 1874 hearings in Albany where her friend Susan Anthony had testified for women's rights. The new Adirondack Railway from Saratoga had only recently reached North Creek, making travel easier and more comfortable for those with business in the mountains. She settled into an empty seat at the back of the car and looked out at the large Saratoga station.

From her window seat she watched a man take a young girl's elbow and lead her to the steps where the conductor roared station names on the train's route. The man with the girl had the looks of a Lord Byron hero: pale face, long hair and pouting lips. He held her arm as if reluctant to let her go and appeared to admonish or instruct her while she shook her head; then tore her arm away to board the passenger car. As the train jerked away from the station and its dirty snow, the young woman came down the aisle and reached for the back of a seat to steady her lurching steps.

Heads turned once more, observing the girl's fashionable clothes, the beauty of the heart shaped face and brilliant aquamarine eyes as she searched for a seat. Grace Wickham smiled as the girl approached. The welcoming gesture caused the young woman to pause, look around at the lack of empty places, and bend to ask, "Is this available?"

Grace patted the empty aisle seat. "Please, I'd welcome your company." The station was out of sight now as the train rolled smoothly to the edge of the city.

The girl put her small case on the floor and sat down. Turning to her companion she said in a rush of words, "My name is Genevieve Crane. Mrs. Edward Crane. I'm still getting used to being called Mrs. Crane, so please call me Jenny."

"And I am Grace Wickham." Although she had a year of medical school she chose not to call herself a doctor; but when asked said she was an Herbalist, an herb doctor who preferred nature's remedies. Nor did she offer to be called Gracie as old friends called her, and now her new friend, Ambrose Baldoon, who would be meeting her train in North Creek.

"That was Mr. Crane seeing you off?"

"He's not happy with me leaving," Jenny said. "But he can't refuse me my quest."

"Quest?"

"I'm looking for my brother who is somewhere in the Adirondacks." Jenny carefully removed the matching hat to her burgundy traveling suit as she spoke, placed the fashionable saucer shaped hat on her lap, shook the glossy midnight waves of long hair and said, "There."

"Somewhere in the Adirondacks?"

"I don't mean to sound so vague. He's been in a logging camp. But I believe he intended to leave that and look for work in a tannery. It's just that Lewis himself was vague in the letter."

"There's a tannery where I live in the hamlet of Wevertown. But then there are many in the Adirondacks." Gracie wondered about the vagueness of Jenny's plan. Did she have one?

2

"I'll go to the end of the line in North Creek and begin my search in that neighborhood. It's important that I find him." Before Gracie could ask or consider whether it was her business to probe, Jenny went on.

"A fortune teller told me he's far away, but I knew that. And in a séance in Saratoga I talked with my dead parents, but I can't very well ask Lewis to tell me where he is if he isn't dead."

"You talked with your dead parents?" Gracie suppressed a smile.

"I didn't talk to them directly of course," Jenny demurred. "Not words exactly. Vibrations. When the medium asks the questions you want answers to."

Her hands moved restlessly, smoothing her skirt and picking up and setting down the hat beside her on the padded velvet seat as she went on. "That's what Mrs. Lincoln did, you know, missing her dead little boy."

Gracie shifted in her seat to look out the window so Jenny couldn't see her face. Her frown would have signaled what she thought of the craze for spiritualism and the Fox sisters who started it all with their system of tapping and raps.

Miles passed quickly as Jenny Crane explained the details of her quest and Gracie listened. Jenny was nineteen, married less than a year, and bringing her brother good news if she could find him. They had grown up as orphans on their uncle's farm in Chateaugay outside of Plattsburgh. News of the uncle's death had arrived too late for her to attend his funeral but the solicitor had written to inform her of the inheritance he left his only living relatives, Genevieve and Lewis LaPierre, his sister's children.

"Except that now I'm Mrs. Edward Crane and there's the farm," she said, smoothing her skirt as she spoke. "I expect the farm is something Lewis would be happy to take over." She patted the fashionable reticule to indicate it held the deed she carried with her. "That's why I must find him."

Responding to the anxiety she heard in Jenny's voice, Gracie said, "I hope you do," and turned again to look out the

3

window at the frozen landscape now beginning to melt in places. She wondered if the river ice was breaking up further north. An early spring could mean the log drive down the Hudson would soon begin.

"Are you sure your brother has left the logging camp?" she asked. "Leaving camp before the big drive?"

"Maybe he didn't want to go on it. I don't know what job he held." Her raised voice at the end of her statement made it sound like a question and unsure of what she said.

"Not all the men take part in the log drive," Gracie said.

"I don't know much about it." Jenny colored and went on in an apologetic voice. "First my uncle wrote that Lewis went off suddenly to logging camp. He didn't say but I suspect there was a fuss. That happened more as we grew older. My uncle wasn't used to our questioning his decisions. And..." her voice dropped further. "He wasn't happy about me leaving either." She added, "It became more difficult for Lewis I suspect."

"And you left for Saratoga?"

"Yes. I had a school friend who visited and told me about it. I went back with her and found work at one of the hotels. Congress Hall. Do you know it?"

"I've seen it." Gracie thought it was obvious from her own unfashionable dress, plain dark skirt, white shirtwaist and black wool cape, that Jenny would understand it was not a place she frequented.

The few times Gracie had been to Saratoga she'd gone with her father. She remembered the wide boulevard with hotels rising and of course the grandest of them all, Congress Hall, where Commodore Vanderbilt had chosen to stay. And like all visitors, she and Dr. Wickham had tasted the healing waters of Saratoga, though they hadn't bathed in them as did some.

"Congress Hall is very different from the farm where I grew up," Jenny offered.

"What kind of work did you find?"

"I started as a seamstress. And when the hotel shut down for the winter they kept me repairing linens and laces until I moved up to the dining room the next session. I've been there year round for over two years."

"And that's how you met your husband? The man seeing you off?"

"I met him at the hotel, yes."

Jenny told how her brother had been unable to leave the farm for her wedding and it was three years since she'd seen him. "He's seventeen now. I expect I'll recognize him when I see him though."

"Some changes in those years, I'm sure," Gracie said.

"Oh, he was tall even as a youngster." Jenny took the deed from her reticule and after holding it up, put it back and found her brother's letter. She explained he'd never been big on book learning and that her uncle needed Lewis on the farm, so he only went to school winters.

"Dear Jenny,

This logging camp is not what I expected. Tanning work might suit me better. Will let you know when I get settled.

Your loving brother, Lewis."

"Doesn't give you a lot to go on, does it?" Gracie asked, wondering if Jenny was being foolish or impulsive to be heading off to look for a brother who was maybe seeking tannery work somewhere in the Adirondacks. She could imagine her housekeeper, Hazel, describing Jenny as a flibberty-jibbet.

On the other hand, leaving the farm for work in Saratoga showed an independent streak. But something about Jenny's current plan left Gracie wondering. Was she running away from her new marriage? Was the husband indulging his bride in her adventure but unhappy about it? Conventional wisdom held that married women weren't supposed to go gadding about alone.

"That's the last you heard from your brother?"

Jenny nodded and chose to change the subject. She was full of questions about the new Adirondack Railway. She'd traveled to Saratoga by stagecoach and had never ridden in a train before. The engine noisily pulled the passenger cars along the winding, steep inclines cut between cliffs flanking the Hudson River. As they progressed north, stopping to let passengers off at Hadley, Stony Creek, Thurman, The Glen and Riverside on to the end of the line, Gracie told how Dr. Thomas Durant, president of the Union Pacific railroad brought the new railroad's tracks to North Creek in 1871.

"He's built a home there in the Adirondacks he calls The Gables. He's often out and about. Perhaps you'll see him in North Creek."

"Is there a Mrs. Durant?"

"Yes, but the newspaper said she and the children have remained in England for many years."

"His business must keep him away from his family then?" Jenny asked.

"Edward's business takes him away, too."

Gracie didn't ask what Jenny's husband did and Jenny did not offer as the conductor came through the car calling out the last stop, North Creek. But she wondered about Jenny's brother and his reason for leaving logging camp. That is, if he had.

Two

It was a hell of a night to be fighting a fire at twenty below in your Union suit, the one-piece long-johns they never took off from November until May.

"Fire! Fire!" shouted the foreman, Rudy, as he flung open the door to the lumbermen's dorm, waving his arms like a madman.

"Get your asses out here. Move it!" he hollered, pointing men to the burning cookhouse.

Sleep drugged jacks answered the alarm and staggered out of the bunk house into the nightmare of screaming voices and flames that lit up the black sky.

Disoriented and groggy, unsure of what to do, the men ran helter-skelter, slipping and sliding on the frozen ground. Some struggled to pull on pants and boots as they tumbled out the door into the bone-chilling night.

"Sweet Jesus! Get your boots on. You're no good to me with frozen feet," Rudy roared. The guilty hurried back, knowing every second counted.

Some swore as they rushed to the edge of the burning cookhouse pantry. A few bent to scoop snow in their bare hands and throw it uselessly at the blaze.

One man stumbled too close to the fire, igniting the blanket he'd wrapped himself in. Another tackled him to the ground to smother the flames the man hadn't been aware of. The underdressed men ignored the artic air that made them shiver

7

even as they edged close to the fire, but each breath burned their throats as a reminder to damn the cold.

A burning shingle flew off, hitting a man rushing toward the fire. Another man dashed to him to smother the missile with snow, then looked up at the roof, fearing more flaming arrows. He reached over for his friend and struggled to drag him across the frozen ground to safety. "Watch it!" he cried, warning off the stampede of men bent on saving the building; a fire within each man to quench the fire they faced. How in God's name had it started?

A light wind licked the fire adding fuel to the searing flames as the men hurried to douse them. All the attached buildings and equipment from weeks and months of intensive labor would be lost if they didn't stop the spreading inferno. At some point each man considered the stored dynamite that could send them all rocketing skyward to eternity.

Rudy cursed and yelled again, trying to bring some order to the ineffectual efforts of his crew. "Form a line to the river. I want a bucket brigade with anything that'll hold water. Break the ice with your axes and start haulin' water up here. And be quick about it!" he commanded.

Within minutes a line snaked from the skidway where cut logs stood stacked along the water's edge; men smashing ice to get at water. They hurriedly passed anything that could hold ice chunks or snow or icy water to those throwing it at the building's flames. Sparks arced the night like fireworks; the hiss and crackle of burning wood forming the background to shouts and curses that sounded like an orchestra gone mad.

Clouds pushed by a southwest wind parted to reveal a three quarter waning moon as the flames rose higher lighting up the sky, and the men got a clearer look at what they'd been fighting.

"Holy shit! There's somebody in there! Look, he's dancing around! Swinging—what the hell?" It was Paddy Somerville shouting. He'd come late fall with the rest of the men to lay out the roads and set up the lumber camp north of Indian Lake. Paddy grabbed a bucket of snow turned slushy from the heat of the fire and threw it on the hanging body to keep it from burning beyond recognition. He wanted to be able to identify who it was. Inform the family.

Men who tired of camp life, the hard work of putting up the buildings: the dormitory where they slept, the dining room, the office, the company store; cutting selected trees into the required 13 x 6 logs, marking them as Newtown's lumber, dragging them to the skidway—some of those tired men just walked out for home when they had enough. But this was different; this one chose another way to leave Newtown's Camp.

In the following days the loggers would talk about that. Who was he? Why had he hung himself? Did he plan the fire, too? How many would know his name? What crew did he work with? Some would try to remember what they knew about him. Had he talked about family?

From the shelter of tall balsams at the edge of the camp a lone figure watched the men he knew work to put out the flames. The cookhouse pantry was off limits to all but the cook and his assistant but it had served his purpose earlier. He'd propped the body against a wall inside and lowered the rope around the neck; thrown the end over a meat hook holding a slab of bacon so the body could swing. It was to have looked like a suicide but when the candle flame caught the papered box, what had it mattered if the body burned.

Wouldn't you know it'd be Paddy Somerville who'd see him swinging there. Loud mouthed Paddy, always letting you know he'd run away to war as a kid. Paddy and his bragging.

Now he could smell burning meat, beef carcasses that'd been hanging on hooks, dripping animal fat ignited by flames, the sound of cans popping like rifle shots.

He walked further from the cookhouse and the men who battled to save it as he thought of what to do next. There'd been no time to think when the nosey bastard discovered what he was doing. The punk could have ruined the whole plan.

It was a good plan; he'd done what he set out to do. The beauty of it was no one suspected. Sure it was a gamble, but he was used to taking risks. Tell me a law that isn't made to be broken if you weren't afraid to risk it.

Now what? There were thousands of acres in the Adirondacks where a man could get lost. But he couldn't leave now. It would look suspicious. He'd have to slip back and help fight the fire. No, he'd leave when it suited him.

Three

Sitting in the high ceiling room of Saratoga's Congress Hall, the two men hidden by tall, potted palms ignored the string quartet playing at the far end of the marble floored dining room. They were in an expansive mood as over coffee and cordials they discussed how to improve their growing business selling Dr. Crane's Golden Medicine Discovery.

"We need testimonials, Eddie. Testimonials from happy customers."

Edward frowned at the nickname, interrupting his own musings about how better to promote the wondrous balm he brought to sufferers. "What about before and after pictures on our hand bills?" He wasn't sure how this was done without some careful editing but he wanted Galvin Swagger to know he had ideas, too. Matthew Brady's Civil War photos had opened the way to more photography used in business.

With a wave of his large paw-like hand his partner dismissed him and growled in a deep rasp. "No, no. Testimonials! Important people. Or someone brimming with health, Eddie. Health from our product."

"Brimming?" Edward wondered how someone brimmed.

The new dining room hostess crossed the busy room at that moment, leading an elderly couple to their table. Here was a natural beauty with a face that belonged on a coin. Her straight posture, clear skin, bright eyes, and long jet black curls only added to the overall impression of curvaceous ripeness. The two men watched the rest of the room follow the hostess with

11

their eyes. If others wondered who she was, to Galvin Swagger they were seeing a walking testimonial of what Dr. Crane's Golden Medicine Discovery could do. She brimmed.

With Swagger standing in as best man and sharing the rented Saratoga mansion with the happy couple, Genevieve LaPierre and Edward Crane were married after a whirlwind courtship. Edward was smitten with his bride and stunned at his good fortune.

At the moment, however, just how happy the couple was seemed in doubt. The senior partner had only recently returned from a supply trip to New York and heard for the first time of a wrinkle in their plans from a nervous Eddie.

Swagger frowned. "What do you mean? She's not cooperating?" He brushed off the fallen ash, dislodging the collected bits of paper and string in his chest pocket, and shoved them haphazardly back; a pack rat who never threw anything away.

"Restless. Got some wild idea about setting off to find her brother."

"He's lost?"

"She's got a letter. At least she says she got a letter from him.

"She got a letter," Swagger rasped. "So what?"

"She wants to tell him about the farm. What the uncle left them."

"Let her write him then."

"Says she can't. He's leaving the logging camp."

"Am I missing something?"

"She wants to go searching for the brother."

"Tell her no. We have commitments." He rumbled on. "Or we'll have her committed." When he saw the look on his partner's face he became annoyed and growled, "Just kidding."

"She's no fool, Swagger. I'm inclined to let her have her quest as she calls it."

"Let me talk to her."

"You can't. She's already left."

"Does she know she's supposed to go with you to Rochester in three weeks?" His tone implied, "How could you let this happen?" Although Jenny did nothing but sit on the stage while Eddie charmed his audience, Swagger smelled loss of control in this latest news

"She'll be back in time. How many tanneries can there be in the Adirondacks?" Edward asked.

"That's where she's going?"

"Says that's where her brother was headed to look for work."

"You believe her?"

"That's the problem. I'm not sure."

Four

Gracie had wired her arrival time, anticipating Ambrose would meet her. From the train's window she saw him waiting at the station; a well dressed man, as befit the proprietor of Baldoon's Hotel, and one of the few men taller than her six feet. He stood beside his shining Joubert and White buckboard, the gleam of the polished wood like the gleam of its owner's bald head and wide smile.

After hours spent in the overheated passenger car, the biting cold night air hit the women like sleet battering their faces. Jenny stood aside, hands in her muff, while introductions were made. "Is someone meeting you?" Ambrose asked the girl.

"It's a long story, Ambrose," Gracie answered for her. "Perhaps we could see Jenny to her hotel."

Ambrose Baldoon looked more like a General Washington than a General Grant, his West Point classmate. Taller than the average man and weighing two hundred and forty pounds, he cut an imposing figure. His fair brows sat over clear, bright blue eyes. There was a dusting of snow on the shoulder of his dark coat and with the pleasure of seeing him again Gracie had to resist the temptation to touch him by brushing it away. It would be too forward in public.

Along with other departing passengers, the women stepped between dirty snow banks and followed Ambrose to his vehicle where he stowed Gracie's small, paisley valise, a typical carpet bag carried by women at the time. It held her change of under things to be washed out each night, extra black stockings, two shirtwaists, a nightgown and toiletries. In addition she'd enclosed two small books for reading: one on herbs and the other of Shakespeare sonnets. She carried her journal in her reticule where she'd jotted notes from the legislative hearing.

Jenny followed closely, like a chick following a mother hen, watching the big man place Miss Wickham's valise in the back seat of his vehicle. Gracie suspected Jenny might be having second thoughts about setting off alone in the Adirondacks now that she'd arrived at the end of the line.

As they walked the short distance to The American hotel, Ambrose suggested they have dinner there before the five mile return to Wevertown. "I'd planned to invite you, anyway, Gracie. I like to see what my competition is up to."

She accepted his offered arm and smiled as she agreed. "It might help Jenny to settle in if we had dinner with her."

While they waited for Jenny to see her room, she told Ambrose the little she'd learned of the girl's personal history and of the intended search for the brother.

"There were just the two of them that the uncle took in when their parents died. She hasn't seen her brother in some time and wants to tell him of their inheritance. Says she's newly married and I believe the man I saw seeing her off is her husband." She thought of Jenny's silence on what her husband did for a living.

"Well, let's hope she finds her brother quickly. She's too attractive and young to be wandering around alone."

"I have an uneasy feeling all is not as it appears on the surface, Ambrose. But I hesitate to pry."

When Jenny returned they entered the crowded dining room where Ambrose pointed to Dr. Thomas Durant sitting at a white covered table with another man.

Ambrose held a chair for Jenny and told her who Durant's guest was. "Andrus Otis. One of the lumber barons from Glens Falls. He owns Newtown Loggers as well as other properties.

Most people would go to him. But he had to come to North Creek if he wanted to see Durant."

Jenny stood to go over to where the lumber baron sat with Durant just as Gracie restrained her by gently placing a hand on her arm.

"But maybe he can tell me about my brother," Jenny pleaded.

"Mr. Otis wouldn't know the workers in his camps," Gracie told her. "He hires contractors called jobbers who take a crew in to erect the camp and run it. I doubt if Mr. Otis has ever been inside one of his logging camps."

Jenny sighed her disappointment as she took her seat again and from the white-aproned waitress accepted a platter-size menu offering trout, fried chicken, venison, beef stew, and kidney pie. She glanced at Mr. Baldoon who was looking at Miss Wickham in an admiring way.

Jenny's curiosity about her new friend and the big man meeting her didn't last long as she put down her menu, thinking again of her brother. "Does Dr. Durant own a tannery or lumber camp, too, Mr. Baldoon?"

"When you bring tracks through you acquire land on either side, some of it good for lumbering," Ambrose answered.

"He also has a saw mill and woodworking plant here, but I don't think he owns the tannery," Gracie added. "That would be Milton Sawyer and whoever his latest partner is."

"Otis owns several timber operations so my guess is it's the saw mill they'll be discussing," Ambrose said. "I recommend the trout, Jenny. Now tell me what your plans are for finding your brother."

They chose the fish with garlic potatoes and candied carrots and Gracie agreed to a glass of sherry with Ambrose. While she shared many of Susan Anthony's views on rights for women, she had not joined the Temperance movement where many of Susan's supporters could be found.

After dessert Jenny appeared in better spirits, agreeing that the hotel's reputation for apple pies was well deserved. As they bid the girl good night, Ambrose returned to Jenny's problem.

"If you're looking for your brother in a tannery, there's one in North Creek at Mill Pond, walking distance from here." He pulled a card from the vest pocket that held his chained gold watch and gave his business card to Jenny. "But in case you don't find your brother in North Creek and decide to come to Wevertown, you'll want to stay at Baldoon's. The stage makes a regular stop." They said their goodbyes and left the hotel.

Outside the two friends settled in Ambrose's buckboard under bearskin lap robes for warmth. Metal runners replaced the wheels for the winter, turning the vehicle into a sleigh. The horse, its breath rising in a frosty plume, turned into the night toward Wevertown. Stars brightened the clear, cold sky, and soon Gracie sighted the nearby Hudson River.

"I see the river, Ambrose." Her breath hung white each time she spoke. The night was cold but that would soon change in the days ahead and the log drive would begin. With that in mind she said, "Did you know the loggers pull in from the drive to overnight at The Glen, and neighbors bring food and join them? I hope you'll come this year."

He turned to look at her, making little clouds with his own words. "I've already had an invitation from John Dillon."

"Really?" She smiled. Dillon supervised the annual river drive that sent the Adirondack logs to market and was viewed as a capable but reticent man. But Ambrose had a gift for making friends since he'd come to Wevertown a little over three years ago and revived the old hotel a few yards from her home.

"While you were gone, Gracie, I went with John to some of the camps that will soon be sending down their logs."

"He must think a lot of you to take you along."

"I volunteered. Last year Nexus North sent more logs down than usual and he wondered if they would again this year so we stopped there. I was curious to see the operations for myself."

Gracie mused aloud, "Addie nearly married that jobber at Nexus North, Tom Stockton. But John Dillon's the better man."

"That explains Stockton's attitude," Ambrose said. "Suspicious of why Dillon was there. Arrogant sort of fellow. But if he was courting Addie Dillon at one time, no wonder they bristled like two polecats."

Gracie's thoughts shifted to who would be moving the logs. She said, "The Somerville boys should be at The Glen when the drive arrives for an overnight."

"You couldn't know, Gracie. Sam's back home."

"Why?"

"Kate took sick and couldn't drive the team anymore so Sam left camp and is back."

She sat upright and dropped the lap robe from her chin to ask, "How sick? Is she going to be all right?"

"From what I heard, yes." He turned to look at her. "If I know you, you'll probably want to run out to the farm to see her."

"I like all of the Somervilles, but especially Kate."

"She's the one taught in the Wevertown School?"

"Before she was replaced, yes. Kate wasn't much older than the boys who came during the winter session when farm chores are over. Apparently the school trustees feared there might be discipline problems and replaced her with a man. But she wants to further her education and needs money to go to the Glens Falls Academy."

Ambrose shook his head. "Somehow she'd convinced her brother Sam to go to lumber camp and let her drive the team."

"I'll check myself to see how Kate's doing. Bring her something. If Sam is home from Newtown logging camp, maybe the Somerville boys knew Jenny's brother before he left."

"Are you taking up Jenny's search?" Ambrose teased.

"We may never see her again, but if she does come here..."

Ambrose drew the horse and sleigh to a stop at the horse block in front of the large Wickham house so Gracie could step down into the cold night. Kerosene lamps gave off warm light through the frosted panes to welcome her home.

Five

"Welcome home, Miss Wickham." It came not from her housekeeper but Hazel's cousin, Margaret Moloney.

Standing behind Margaret, Hazel's scowl revealed she wanted to be the first to welcome her employer. Now she stepped forward to scold. "Close the door. You're letting all the cold in. Here. Let me have your things."

Obadiah, the marmalade cat sitting in the plum colored lady's chair, failed to rise in welcome, letting Gracie know what he thought about her leaving him. Gracie smiled with affection at her white-haired housekeeper. "I'm glad to see you, too, Hazel." Hazel had come to them when Doctor Wickham's wife became ill and Miss Wickham had been "little Gracie." Hazel still called her Gracie.

She handed Hazel her black cloak, patted Obadiah's head, and rubbing her hands together briskly marched into the kitchen to have a cup of tea, followed by the two cousins eager to hear of her Albany trip. News from out of town came in the weekly paper the *Warrensburg News* that Gracie wrote for occasionally, but now they would hear from the local correspondent herself. One reason for the trip to Albany, in addition to supporting Susan, was her assignment to write about the legislation's hearings.

She held the cup for its warmth as she told them about Susan Anthony's plea for women's rights before the state legislature. Knowing both women disapproved of what they

19

called such shenanigans, she quickly moved on to tell of the train ride and the young woman she'd met.

"She's looking for her brother somewhere here in the Adirondacks. Thinks he left logging camp to find work in a tannery."

Hazel said, "Here in Wevertown?"

"She's not sure. All he wrote was that logging wasn't what he wanted."

Margaret, who never let information go by without adding to it, warmed to what she knew of the horrors of logging from neighbors who'd lost husbands or sons. "Remember Lizzie Tibbets' boy, Hazel? Drivin' to the skidway and squashed when the sled got goin' too fast and he didn't jump off in time? And Sara Ordway's man killed by a tree snappin' back." Margaret hugged her plump arms to her chest and added, "Widow-maker's the right name for sure."

Hazel looked at her employer helplessly. Her cousin's loquaciousness on any subject tried Hazel's patience and without Miss Wickham's calm presence these past days, her temper had been sorely tested. Gracie knew March weather contributed to people's ediginess and expected to pay for her time away with a number of grouchy patients waiting at her doorstep. She just hadn't expected it within her own home.

Hazel was a neat, sensible woman, organized in her thoughts and words and appearance. Margaret's appearance reflected her scattered thoughts. Streaked grey hair in danger of escaping the bun at the top of her head; buttons straining across her ample bosom, her animated face constantly flushed, anticipating all she had to say.

Margaret heedlessly went on clucking. "Young man's smart to get out and find less dangerous work in a tannery."

Margaret conveniently forgot the fatal accidents that occurred in tanneries and the death of her late employers. Hazel took pride in her employer's reputation for helping others, including welcoming Margaret who no longer had a position and place to live, and had not yet found another housekeeping job

Throughout the evening they heard of every danger and death Margaret knew of and intended to share on what could happen in a logging camp. Of "fool killers," those saplings that caught and bent over, making them into deadly coiled springs and named for the foolish who didn't watch where they walked. Of someone's son who forgot to walk on the uphill side of a log when driving his horse.

Tired from her journey and Margaret's litany of logging tragedies, Gracie looked at her father's gold watch on its chain against her chest and yawned. "Let's hope all those dire accidents don't appear in our dreams," and with a smile bid them good night.

Glad to be home in her own bed, Gracie slept soundly that night, falling asleep to the roar of a swollen Mill Creek behind the tannery across the road. In the morning Hazel fussed over her breakfast in the unspoken way she welcomed her mistress' return by making fresh doughnuts. Dripping icicles outside the kitchen window gave evidence ice was breaking up and lumbermen would be getting the logs started for the drive south. Hazel was melting, too, no longer muttering about Grace Wickham's foolishness for going to Albany to support that misguided Susan Anthony.

The tannery teamsters had switched their box wagons from sleds to wheels, another sign of spring, although the road was still ice-rutted in places. Gracie left the front window and returned to the kitchen where Hazel had her arms in a sink full of suds, attacking wet kitchen towels on a small scrub board. Margaret sat at the table sorting the silverware and muttering to herself of lumbering accidents like someone's lost husband struck in the head by a falling limb from a huge birch he'd just cut down. Hazel turned to look at Margaret and in a voice that could freeze the dripping icicles outside, answered the last tragedy with, "Yes, Margaret. We know you know all about camp life."

Since Gracie returned with the story of Jenny Crane's brother leaving logging for other work, Margaret's memory of multiple horror stories of logging accidents, fatal and otherwise, had been revived. Few women were willing to endure cooking prodigious meals for forty or fifty lumberjacks in the isolated setting of a lumber camp. Camp cooks were usually men. But the pay was good and Margaret had once been the cook at Nexus North for a season.

"Know it first hand, anyways," Margaret sniffed.

Gracie interceded. "Ambrose said he met Tom Stockton when he went out to Nexus North, Margaret. He was there when you were cook, wasn't he?"

"Yes. Moody man he was. Suspect it was the drink."

"I thought drinking was discouraged," Gracie said.

"It was. Too dangerous in the woods and not allowed in camp. But he was the camp boss and what he did away from the men...." She thought a moment and added, "Think that Frenchy fella was a bad influence, but he took off in mid season. Who knows where."

Gracie looked at Hazel who shook her head to indicate she didn't know what Margaret was talking about.

"He was tolerable long as he didn't get in my way. In my kitchen."

Was Margaret talking about Tom Stockton or Frenchy? Whoever he was, it seemed all the Canadians loggers were called Frenchy whether they spoke French or not. Gracie wondered briefly if Margaret had ever seen the antagonism between Tom Stockton and John Dillon, but decided against repeating what Ambrose had said about that. Her own kitchen had enough dissension between the two cousins and she was grateful Hazel hadn't come up with a tart remark about whose kitchen they were in.

"I'll be in the back office if anyone needs me," she said and escaped to the privacy of her professional space.

After Gracie had seen her last patient on her first full day home, the three women sat at the round kitchen table finishing their meal of venison stew and gravy biscuits. From a rafter hung bundled herbs. The breath and smells of the large country house came daily from breads baking in the huge oven, or soups and herbal decoctions and infusions simmering on the cook top. In the much used kitchen a three sided pie-cupboard stood in one corner, with a tall wooden rocker nearby that held yarns of knitting wool left in the seat. The wind howled down the chimney, causing the coals to redden and move at the bottom of the cook stove. Hazel stood and threw in another piece of wood and returned to the table, saying she couldn't eat another bite.

Margaret turned from the stove where she added seconds to her bowl as if she hadn't heard Hazel's remark and plumped herself down in the chair for emphasis.

"Remember Mabel Higgins' husband? Riding on top of all those logs on the icy slope and too late jumping off when they got going too fast." She paused long enough to swallow what was on her spoon and said, "Crushed like a bed bug he was." She looked at Miss Wickham. "Luck of the draw, his uncle said."

Searching to distract her, Gracie asked if they'd heard about Kate Somerville. "While Sam was in logging camp Kate's been driving the family wagon carrying bark to the tannery. To earn tuition money for the academy. Ambrose said when she took sick, Sam came home."

Margaret finished her stew and giving her opinion of each member, fastened on the farm family of the Somervilles. "Paddy's the cut-up. Comes from being the middle one, I 'spose. Ran off underage to fight with the Union, looking for glory."

She recounted each prank and devilment he created as a youngster. She dismissed the youngest son, Sam, as having the sensibility of a puppy, and Kate as too ambitious by far wanting to go to the Glens Falls Academy when the family couldn't afford it since the father's death. That led her to the unusual death of the father who died from lockjaw through a small, infected cut.

The other two knew the story but Margaret told it again. "Said he had to check on the land. Shouldn't have shaved before he set down to eat his noon meal." Margaret shook her head at his foolishness. "Suffered somethin' awful he did, poor man."

Hazel pursed her lips like she was sucking a lemon when Margaret predicted more doom for the Somervilles, "Pray no misfortune comes to that rascal, Paddy, on the log drive."

As she listened half-heartedly to Margaret's opinions, Gracie considered what kind of a tonic she could bring to the recovering Kate. She'd learned about the uses of herbs from her father who told her that from the time of Hippocrates the first physicians had all been herbalists. But it was her mother who tended the garden and taught her from an early age the names and care of all the plants. Maybe Elderberry? Burdock? She would choose something from one of the many small glass bottles neatly arranged on the shelves in her office.

She stood and carried her dish to the sink. "I think I'll drive out to see Kate Somerville tomorrow."

Margaret looked startled at the news and waited to hear if they would be invited to ride along, but Gracie thinking of her father's saying, 'some books are better left on the shelf,' issued no invitation.

"I'll go alone this time and find out just how sick Kate has been, and if she's up to having visitors."

Hazel glared at her cousin as if it was her fault they hadn't been invited to ride along. But Margaret simply shrugged and returned to thinking about logging camp. Talking to herself in reminiscence about "that Frenchy fella you couldn't trust," she missed the look supposed to silence her.

Six

Nexus North lay deep in the Adirondacks west of Newcomb where Margaret had once been camp cook. It was there Tom Stockton sat in his private quarters away from the men in their dormitory, nursing the whiskey forbidden to his working jacks. A thick dark beard and side chops covered youthful acne scars but years of drinking had ruined whatever good looks he'd had. He was short but had a muscular, burly body with curly black hair and caterpillar eyebrows over gimlet black eyes. He kept running his hands through his hair as if it could keep him from thinking of tomorrow.

Knowing that Johnny—Superintendent John Dillon—was due to come to camp the next day, Tom had decided to turn in early and now killed the kerosene lamp, only to toss and turn before the recurring nightmare returned. Once again the two friends faced off for a knock down fight after a misunderstanding that lasted the rest of their lives.

They fought with bare knuckles, swearing and yelling, taunting, kicking, tearing at the other's clothes, swiping away bloody noses, finally wrestling on the bare ground until Johnny reached for the stick they'd rolled onto.

In his dream, Tom once more tore it from his hands and stood up swinging, again and again, as Johnny ducked each time. Tom swinging the stick in a mad frenzy, swinging with bile in his throat; swinging and missing until he was tripped by Johnny, and laying there bruised and bleeding, unable to get up, watched Johnny walk away.

"You men, here. Count off. I need ten to cut spruce I've marked." He could handle the routine of his days. "I'll look for you—all of you..." he counted with his sharp eyes what looked to be twenty-five in the group waiting for his order, "...look for you to get the cut logs to the banking grounds."

Tom had done it all over the years cutting, building crib damns, scaling timber, branding logs and finally the big drive, giving orders as the Nexus camp boss. But it was Johnny who won again when he'd become the overall boss and Superintendent of the river drive.

Hung over and hoping it didn't show, Tom squinted into the sunshine the next morning. Two men waited for him down at the skidway. Superintendent Dillon was looking at the logs stored there and turned to introduce the big man he brought with him.

Tom stood listening scornfully, his big hands close fisted at his sides as Johnny talked. Tom's dark scowl was meant for the former friend who'd become his nemesis.

Dillon stood with his hands on his hips looking around at the logs chained in place, then turned to the visitor. "Each company has its own mark, Ambrose."

He'd invited the hotel proprietor to ride out with him to see the lumber operation at Nexus North.

"Can be a square, a diamond, a star, a triangle or..." he paused, "letters like the big N for Newtown," Dillon pointed. "Here's Nexus North. Their logs are identified by what some think is a crude butterfly. See?"

"H-m-m." The big man fingered the mark. "And you do this so...?"

Tom thought the man was just being polite for God's sake. What reason could there be?

He saw the Superintendent's confident smile as he answered, "Once measured and branded with their special design by the marking hammer we can identify who it belongs to at the end of the drive." His hand rested on the branded log as he looked at Tom.

"The law requires this?" the big man asked.

26

Tom spoke up. "As of 1825. Passed by the state legislature." He knew the history of logging as well as Johnny Dillon.

He studied Johnny. Was he remembering they'd once been best friends when they'd fished and hunted together, and at thirteen set off to earn a living in the woods. Did he ever think about the fight that ended it? The superintendent's face was all business, revealing nothing.

Tom breathed a sigh of relief when the two visitors left. He hadn't liked the way the conversation was going. And Johnny had come right out and said he was interested in how many logs Tom thought they'd cut. That made him sweat. He watched them get into the wagon that would take them out of camp on rutted roads back to civilization.

He had a lot to think over as he walked back to the office. Where was Jacques now? He'd like to tell him about this morning's visit. Tom owed his life to Jacques Girard two seasons ago when the young man pushed him out of the way just as a widow maker snapped back. In return he offered him a drink that night and invited the dark haired logger to his cabin by way of thanks.

From then on it was the grin that the little bastard used when you gave orders or dressed him down; as if it didn't matter whether you praised him or cursed him. Then that day at work's end when he caught up to Tom and said, "I'll arm wrestle you for a cool one." God, the brass on the kid but his cockiness made Tom laugh and look around before he said, "Yes, but in my quarters."

After that, Jacques invited himself in the evening when he felt like it and Tom admitted to himself the kid was company as they drank and talked. Jacques could be funny mimicking the other French Canadians and laughing at himself as well. He even did an imitation of the camp cook, Margaret, and her habit of nosey questions. Puffing himself up and waddling around the room nodding his head as she did and capturing Margaret's voice. "And you're a good friend of Mr. Stockton's,

27

young Jacques?" That sobered Tom. Was he seen as playing favorites?

Still, Tom let himself be drawn in by Jacques' humor; his light heartedness so different from Tom's darkness. It wasn't long before Tom poured out his troubles with each glass. One night he told Jacques the mitten story and of his father's repeated advice, another painful memory that surfaced in Tom's nighttime dreams.

He was thirteen again and his family expected him home for Easter before the log drive began. When he asked the head man for his pay, he'd been handed a pair of logger's mittens.

"This is all I get?"

"There's no money," the man told him. "Not 'til the end of the drive."

His father's stern voice was always the same with the lecture he gave Tom. "Let that be a lesson for you to be honest. Work hard. Work so you're the boss."

Jacques frowned. "Honest? Work hard? So that's what this is all about? What's it get you, Tom?" Jacques had asked and sneered. He waved his long simian arms in the air as he said, "All this straight and narrow stuff, playing by the rules."

Tom weighed Jacques' youthful rebellious and his challenging voice as he talked about rules and laws and how there's always a way to get around them.

That's how it began. Jacques convinced him he'd found a way they could both profit, insisting, "I'll be the one taking the risk, Tom."

Looking back, he knew that was the night they'd become more than drinking friends. But now Tom was nervous about this season. He didn't need another inspection.

When had he stopped taking risks, Tom wondered? At nineteen, he'd been as reckless and daring as any young man on the water. Had told his Addie what he'd done, out there on the river and watched her eyes shine at his daring.

"Right in the middle of the rapids, holding on to a slippery boulder, Old Bill was in trouble," he'd explained. "Couldn't have lasted in that freezing water. I jumped on a log, rode into white water, swept past the rock, grabbed Bill by the collar and hauled him clear."

"Just like that?" she'd asked. Addie had hung on his every word and Tom thought they had an understanding.

He hadn't hesitated to say, "Ask Johnny. He was there. He can tell you."

Johnny Dillon had told Addie something, but it wasn't the story of Tom's rescue of a stranded logger. Did Johnny think Tom pushed him into that jam when he'd jumped on the log to go after the helpless man? He remembered Johnny yelled, "Wait. What are you doing?"

Johnny to this day probably thinks I pushed him away when I reached out to haul Bill. Couldn't stand it I left him to save that man. Must have told a different version to cause Addie to send her sister to the door to say she didn't want to see me ever again.

Tom shook his head at the painful memories that seeing Johnny again always brought and walked back to the office. Somehow he got through the rest of the day, his head throbbing and feeling he needed a drink. He staggered carefully to the kerosene lantern he'd placed on the floor by his bunk and clutching the bottle clumsily, began taking off his boots. He reached over and turned down the wick of the lantern by his cot, pulled the blanket over the clothes he slept in and lay back hoping the nightmare wouldn't find him tonight.

The gong would wake him soon enough for another day in this godforsaken hell of a job. Dillon would soon give the word to open the skidway. Then it would begin. The whole water system would be opened, like veins leading to arteries, emptying into the source. The river of life for the drive. The Hudson.

But this time when the logs reached Glens Falls, Tom knew he'd take his bonus and clear out.

Seven

As Gracie set off along the road to the Somerville farm, tall pine branches glistened with thin ribbons of snow from the evening's dusting. Bare limbs of dark maples invited black capped chickadees to celebrate the morning sunshine in frenzied acrobatic swoops, and patches of snow and melting ice could be seen in nearby fields.

Somerville Road, like many in the town, came from the name of the family who lived there. When The Glen tannery burned, John Somerville had been given land for his lost wages. Over the years the farm had grown to a compound of buildings: the original house with its additions, the barn, smoke house and other outbuildings, and then the new house across the brook when the eldest son, Johnny, married Emma, who'd come to teach at the one-room Somerville school. Grown maples on either side of the short driveway led to the barn where a dog bounded out barking at the intruder.

"Miss Wickham!" the oldest son greeted her as he took the reins of her horse. "You've come to check on Kate?"

The dog continued barking and ran toward her, his tail wagging his welcome as well. She guessed it was a mix of Labrador and Golden Retriever, its coat a muddy gold of flopping welcome.

"I have." Gracie stepped down and let Kate's brother take care of her buggy as she patted the dog's head.

"That's enough Goldie," the owner said when the dog sniffed her skirt and was pulled away.

When she entered the farmhouse, the glare from the bright sun on snow made her eyes water and it took a moment to adjust to the dim rooms inside. She almost tripped on the piece of horseshoe nailed to the threshold of the door that guarded against the influence of fairies. Kate's parents had both come from Ireland, bringing the custom that kept sprites from entering their home.

Under her woolen cloak the cuttings from her window pots had been protected and now Gracie carried them in her cold hands. Kate's mother led her up the narrow stairway after thanking Miss Wickham for the tonic she'd brought. She had considered several different kinds of tonics: too early for rhubarb and nettle, unless she could find a bush winter-protected by a spruce tree. Nettle tea was good for Margaret's arthritis but Gracie had finally decided on Pennyroyal, growing in a window pot, and made an infusion by bruising the leaves. Before leaving her house she sweetened it with honey to make it more appealing. She reasoned an energizing tonic would do no harm and see for herself Kate's condition.

The sick girl was sitting up in bed, pale but happy to see her visitor. Kate put her nose in the bouquet of herbs Miss Wickham presented and happily sniffed the sprigs of rosemary, sage and thyme, chosen for their pungent smell. Kate was even thinner than before. She looked like a plucked chicken from the loss of her hair due to high fever, and just now growing back. Considered a tomboy, but as Margaret would say, "What can you expect with all those brothers?"

Gracie thought Kate was rather pretty, and she certainly identified with the girl's desire for an education. It had not been certain Kate would survive the typhoid fever and even less certain how she'd contracted it. Gracie heard of no other cases. She pulled a chair close to Kate's bed and asked, "You hauled bark this winter?"

"I did, Miss Wickham." There was pride in her voice as Kate answered.

31

"What was that like?"

"Well, after chores I hitched up the team and set off to pick up the bark and load it on the sled." Kate smiled at her ready listener.

"How many cords?"

"My arms ached from loading two or three."

"Wore yourself out, sounds like, out there in the cold?" Gracie asked with a concerned look.

"The effort warmed me, actually. Sitting on top of the bark I thought of hot summer days and the berries I like to pick. It wasn't so bad," she finished.

"Bad enough." Gracie patted Kate's hand. "I brought you some pennyroyal tonic since I wasn't sure just how you were."

"Saw you at Christmas but what with all those people we didn't stay long." Kate changed the subject. "Paddy and Sam were home for the holiday and wanted to see the hotel's new gas lighting."

Ambrose had spent the fall months having indoor gas lights installed for his Christmas party and many of the locals had never seen this new convenience. The new lamps now lit up the hotel's corner and an unusual number of vehicles of all kinds had parked there during the winter months. Business had increased even beyond what Ambrose had already accomplished in renovating the old hotel.

Kate looked away and lowered her voice. "And now Sam's home for good."

"I was surprised he went in the first place."

The girl's face colored and there was a quick moistening of her lips before she returned to sniffing the herbs. "He didn't want to go, but I needed tuition money so he let me drive the team. I know he's glad to be out of that camp."

Gracie searched for something positive to say. "I'm sure Paddy liked showing his younger brother around."

"I suppose. But Sam never did adjust. Logging's not for everyone. And shortly before he left camp, there was a suicide."

"Someone they knew?"

"I don't think so."

"Some family will be grieving, I'm sure." Gracie cast about for a more cheerful topic, and began with her trip to Albany.

"Susan has returned to speaking to lawmakers across the country on the need to protect women's rights. Her argument is the unfairness of laws made only by men, for men, and executed by men. Susan believes, given the chance to make their own fortunes, as she says, 'it would give women an equal chance in money getting.'"

Kate's eyes glistened and her color heightened as she listened to Miss Wickham's news of the woman who had been arrested for trying to vote in the 1872 election.

"You know, Kate, like you, Susan had an independent spirit even as a girl. She once asked her school teacher why he only taught long division to the boys and she didn't like his answer."

"What did he say?"

"That a girl needs to know how to read the Bible and count her egg money, nothing more."

"That's awful!"

"Well, it was back in the 1830's, although I'm not sure we've made that much progress." Gracie shook her head and went on. "However, you'll like the way Susan got around him...by organizing herself so she sat behind him while he taught the boys and learned long division in spite of him."

Kate laughed and clapped her hands. "That's wonderful!"

Gracie reached over and felt Kate's forehead, wondering if Kate was feverish or beginning to tire. She stood to leave.

Searching for something to cheer Kate further she said, "On the train back I met a young woman whose brother may have been in the same camp as Sam and Paddy." Looking at Kate she described Jenny Crane and why she was in the Adirondacks, then patted Kate's hand once more and said she'd come again. "Perhaps I can bring Jenny if she turns up in Wevertown. See if Sam can tell Jenny anything." Gracie thought a new face close in age to Kate would also be a welcome change from Kate's long days in a sick bed.

33

Outside melting snow was dripping off eaves and branches, sounding like soft wind-blown chimes. Sam was in the yard returning with the wagon for his noon dinner. He was the youngest son, and like all the Somervilles taller than average with curly dark hair, green eyes and the strong family features of chiseled cheekbones and nose. When he wasn't peeling hemlock bark in the woods, Sam drove the team to contribute his earnings to the family.

After exchanging hellos, Gracie greeted him by asking, "How did logging camp go?"

"Can't say I miss it, Miss Wickham." Sam had a boyish grin when he answered. "It's more Paddy's kind of life than mine."

Paddy had once been considered a wild youth who believed his time away as an underage soldier gave him bragging rights when he returned. Another older brother, Robbie, worked in the tannery, and the oldest Somerville son, Johnny, managed the farm.

Paddy was still at the Newtown logging camp and Sam had recently returned so Gracie said, "I met a young woman whose brother may have been at the logging camp when you were there. Thinks he left for work in a tannery and now she's looking for him."

Sam shook his head. "There's more than one man sick of logging at winter's end. Wanting to leave. One way or another." Gracie guessed he was thinking of the suicide.

"Would you know him? Lewis LaPierre?" The sooner Jenny Crane found her brother the safer she'd be.

"Didn't get to know many names. Paddy's the social one in the family." Sam grinned, as if to acknowledge his role as the shy one.

"Well if Lewis LaPierre's sister gets to Wevertown, maybe she can describe her brother and you can tell her what logging camp was like. Her name is Jenny Crane."

As they stood talking, Johnny came from the barn, the dog at his heels, with sap buckets to hang on the tall maple trees that lined the drive.

34

"Not too late to tap?"

"Needed some warm days to get the sap running." He smiled and set the wooden buckets down then looked up at the tall trees. "Looks to be a good year for sugaring."

At that moment Sam's stomach growled loud enough for Johnny to look at him, grin and shake his head. Sam's color rose and Gracie touched his arm and said something told her she should be on her way.

"I'll send word if the young woman who's looking for her brother comes to Wevertown. I'm sure she'll want to talk with someone who was at the same camp."

"Don't see as I can help," Sam said.

She guessed by the look in his eyes that talking to a strange woman would not be Sam's preference. She thought of Jenny's youth and vivacious manner and believed that could put Sam at ease, and he might remember Lewis LaPierre if his sister described him. That is If Jenny hadn't already found him. She wondered if that was the real reason the girl had gone off on her own, leaving her husband back in Saratoga. Something about that felt amiss.

Eight

Back home again, Gracie stood behind her desk in her starched white shirtwaist above a long, black shirt. Her fiery orange hair pulled into a braid at the back of her head brought color to the stark image of her clothes. No one would ever call her a beauty, tall and angular as she was, but her velvet brown eyes shown with kindness from her freckled face. Eyes that reassured patients even before they heard her soft voice asking how she could help.

Some women preferred to see someone of their own sex rather than a male doctor who might live closer. That was true of the Baldwin women from North River now in Gracie's office. Ella Baldwin's low voice rustled like dead leaves underfoot as she presented a jar of clover honey as barter for the office visit.

"It's what my boy Colin makes from his bee hives, Miss Wickham."

Ella was a large woman with the dark skin and planed features that spoke of some Native American heritage. While she used Joe Baldwin's name it was assumed to be a common law marriage because of her Indian blood, considered by some unworthy of legal ties. Belle stood next to Ella, looking like a frail child rather than the mother of the toddler whose hand she held.

"Thank you, Ella. And who do we have here?" Grace stooped to shrink her six foot frame and held out wide arms to the child.

"Jessie's almost two now, Miss Wickham. Go on." Her mother gave a gentle push and the child stepped forward into the open arms to be lifted to Miss Wickham's lap as she returned to her desk chair.

"What can I do for you?" she asked and lifted her father's gold watch from her thin chest to distract the little girl and let her hold it.

"It's the teething we talked about last time," Belle said. "My father-in-law has his own ideas." She bit her lip and looked at Ella as if she needed permission to go on. There was a perceptible nod from Ella. "Well, he's got his own ideas about fixing things. Thinks if we cut Jessie's gums it would relieve the pressure and he wouldn't have to listen to her crying." Belle put a nail bitten finger to her mouth. "We said we'd ask you."

"I'm glad you've come to me. We don't want to do that to this fine lady." Cutting gums was a common practice to ease painful teething, often resulting in making things worse. A dirty knife could cause infection. "Oil of cloves is good for toothache. Hm-m-m. Let's see what we have instead." She handed Jessie to her mother and walked to the shelf where bottles held her syrups, decoctions and remedies.

"Tell me about what's going on near you these days." She pulled a bottle from the shelf and said, "Your farm's not too far from the new garnet mine, is that right?"

"Yes," said Ella.

"Close enough that they want to buy the farm," offered Belle.

"Really!" Gracie turned around, "Here, this may help. It's a mixture of carbolic, spirit of wine, and distilled water. Dampen a small toothbrush or use a clean finger to rub it on her gums to make them less tender. But that tooth will push its way through without anybody cutting her gums."

Belle looked at Ella with what could only be described as a what-did-I-tell-you look and said, "There was an article in Lady

Godey's about carbolic soap and also disinfecting powder. That it can be applied to festering sores or wounds."

"An article or an advertisement?" Gracie asked. "No matter. This is a safe tincture I've put together." She handed the small bottle to Belle.

"How do you feel about selling?" Gracie looked at the women knowing a farm life can be as hard on the women as the men.

"Not ours to decide," Ella said.

"I wish he'd sell," Belle answered. "We could have our own place," she added wistfully. "But my Joe does what his father wants."

Gracie knew Joe Jr. would be in line to inherit as the legal son under the rule of primogeniture. Colin was older but was the boy Ella had before her union with Joe Baldwin. "You also have a younger son, Ella? He works the farm, too?"

"We all do," Belle sighed, ignoring Ella's frown.

"Yes. His name is Ezra."

"He hates the farm," Belle volunteered. "Rather be down at the pub with his pals." She turned to Ella. "It's true, Ma. You know it and it worries you." For such a slight woman Belle had a strong voice.

Gracie asked, "It worries you, Ella?"

"Course." Ella folded her arms across her chest as if to surrender to the obvious.

"It's that Donovan Doyle that Ezra started hanging around with," Belle interjected. "He works in the new mines, and when Ezra's not drinking with him at the pub he hikes himself up to that boarding house to see him. Donny and him get talkin' big about what they could do out west if they had a stake. He tells me about it, hoping I can convince my Joe. That's Ezra's reason to see the farm sold."

"Might it happen?" Gracie asked Ella.

Belle answered, "Never! Already told the land agent no." She looked at Ella and said, "And it were a good price, too, Ma."

Gracie learned a lot about what was going on in the town of Johnsburg from the news her patients brought her. "I haven't seen the garnet mines yet, but I hope to soon."

Belle said, "Well you'll see Ezra plotting his future with Donny Doyle if you stop in at the boarding house they have up there." Belle's look had become a sullen pout as she handed little Jessie to Ella and took the instructions Miss Wickham had written.

As she walked the women out to the parlor, she was surprised to see a familiar figure sitting in the plum colored lady's chair.

"Susan!" Gracie threw open her arms in greeting. The Baldwin women didn't recognize the famous lecturer and let themselves out the front door, for this didn't appear to be a patient waiting to see Miss Wickham.

"I didn't expect to see you so soon."

Susan grasped Gracie's hands and held them to her heart as a sign of affection. "My surprise." The stern face broke into a wide smile. "I thought I'd stop on my way to Plattsburgh."

"You'll be speaking there?"

"Yes. Then across the lake and on to Vermont. Brattleboro, in fact."

"You'll stay the night?"

"I can't. But the train brought me as far as North Creek and you were so close I decided on impulse to see you again. We didn't have much chance to visit in Albany."

"Impulse, Susan?" Gracie smiled. "I don't think that's a word I'd use to describe you!"

Susan left her cloak on the chair and followed Gracie into the kitchen to have tea. After recognizing Miss Anthony at the door, Hazel had taken Margaret with her to the back parlor to give them privacy.

"Impulsive?" Susan laughed. "I've never told you about the time after I met Amelia Bloomer when I cut my hair and decided to wear the comfortable clothes she wore."

"You cut your hair?" Gracie looked at the dark hair parted severely and pulled back into a thick bun at the back of her neck. "The tunic and bloomers, too? You didn't!"

A smiling Susan answered, "This was some time back, you understand. But the ridicule distracted from the message I wanted to get across."

If the stern Susan B. Anthony could ever look sheepish, it was something Gracie believed no one else had ever seen. She reached out to touch Susan's hand across the table. So much hatred and hostility Susan endured from crowds who ridiculed her.

"I've seen a newspaper cartoon of you wearing a top hat with stars and stripes, but not in Amelia Bloomer's clothes."

"Oh, that one. With the umbrella in my hand like a cane? With the hat I look almost as tall as you, my friend."

"What I liked in that cartoon was the man at the side holding the baby."

Susan smiled. "Yes, while all the women were marching. It was certainly better than some I've seen."

"Is it true that Elizabeth's husband said 'You stir up Susan and she stirs up the world'?"

"Yes, he did. Elizabeth and I make a good team. It was Amelia who introduced us at the anti-slavery conference in Syracuse back in 1851. Elizabeth wrote about herself, 'it has been said that I forged the thunderbolts and Susan fires them.'" Susan shook her head. "We thought the Republicans would reward us for building support for the Thirteenth Amendment by giving us the vote. But we were bitterly disappointed."

Gracie saw the deep grooves at the side of Susan's mouth as she spoke, but then Susan lifted her head and the dark eyes sparkled again. "But we soldier on. Failure is impossible."

"That's the Susan that inspires us all," Gracie said, patting Susan's hand again.

"As a matter of fact, that's part of the reason I wanted to see you once more." She reached into her reticule and withdrew a paper. "This is a petition we're circulating. You remember Elizabeth and I wanted a Constitutional

Amendment for our equal rights, but we've joined the others who want to secure the vote through the states. The Wyoming territory has given women the right to vote and we think now that may be the way to go. I'll leave one with you and let you decide what to do with it."

"You know I'll help you if I can. Do you want men to sign it, too?"

"We do have men who support us. Frederick Douglas, of course. Parker Pillsbury, Theodore Tilton."

"I was thinking of the man who owns the hotel where the stagecoach will take you north. His name is Ambrose Baldoon and he's become a friend."

"Why Grace Wickham! Is that a blush?"

"Oh, Susan, you're teasing. I know I'm not blushing." Was she?

"If he's a friend and willing to sign our petition to give women the vote, by all means ask him." Her voice shifted to a sterner tone as she said, "I plead now for the ballot as the great guarantee and the only sufficient guarantee of rights."

"Your Plattsburgh audience will be hearing those words?"

"Yes." Susan sighed and stood. "I must go. I never tire of saying them as I cross the country, although the traveling can be tiring."

They walked to the door where they embraced and said their goodbyes. Gracie stood in the doorway and watched her friend walk to the hotel where she would take the stage. She worried for Susan. While Elizabeth Cady Stanton was confined at home with her children and had the ideas and wrote them, Susan was the one who said them and bore the brunt of antagonistic public opinion. The least she could do was circulate Susan's petition.

Nine

Speculation and rumor about the fire that hellish night eventually played out at the Newtown logging camp. From their rebuilt storeroom and restored supplies the lumberjacks were finishing a breakfast of large helpings. Meals were consumed in silence; the only sounds from the rattling iron spoons and two-tined forks on tin dishes and cups. No man spoke as they consumed mountainous plates of baked beans, salt pork in thick gravy, freshly baked bread, eggs, pancakes, doughnuts and pies.

The men were full in stomach and anticipation as they walked away from their early meal, ready for the most exciting part of lumbering, the river drive. The cook and his assistant, the cookee, along with a blacksmith, would follow with the cook wagon and be ready when the men pulled into shore that evening.

Paddy Somerville belched as he walked beside the young man who'd become his shadow since he'd arrived at camp and began a long explanation of what would soon happen.

"Superintendent Dillon's plan begins by going north to the headwaters to control the farthest body of water first. At each site one unlucky man gets the job of going to the banking grounds below the skidways to loosen the wedge that held the logs in place."

"Unlucky?"

"Yeah, if he doesn't jump out of the way quick enough."

"The drive starts with us?" Paddy was asked.

"Newtown camp isn't the first to get word to release their logs. But once we do, watch out!" Paddy slapped the boy's back for emphasis.

Competition was fierce among logging outfits to be early on the river when it was high and fast, and once word came, the desire was strong to quickly get the logs to Glens Falls. Quickly could be thirty miles a day in high, rushing water, but the haul for many would more likely be a run of two miles a day.

Paddy went on, "The water will be high from the melt after winter's heavy snow and make for a safer run. Low water means scraping rocks and pile-ups."

"You've done the river drive how many times?" he asked Paddy.

"Four."

Before that he'd gone into the woods on one of the gangs. Sometimes cruising for timber, sometimes cutting, loading logs, scaling, willing to do anything until he was allowed to go on the river.

Paddy Somerville at twenty-two had the same good looks as the rest of the Somervilles, tall, curly dark hair and beard, green eyes and a strong face with chiseled looks. Except that Paddy's flattened nose came from a long forgotten fist fight. His broken nose and hot temper set him apart from his family more than anything else.

The eagerness of the young man at his side reminded Paddy that it could have been his brother Sam walking beside him, ready for his first river drive. He had wanted to show Sam what it was like, but Sam left camp before Paddy got the chance and was probably glad to be out of it. Sam would show up with the rest of the family though when they pulled in for the night at The Glen. Everyone would be there. He hoped his sister, Kate, would be well enough to come.

He spoke with pride of his family. "Kate's the youngest, my only sister. Pretty and smart, too. We're all proud of her book learning and how she taught for a while at the Wevertown

43

School. Damn if she doesn't want more schooling—and look what that got her. Working so hard to earn tuition money and now sick with something nobody else caught, looks like."

Well, he'd show her off to his new friend. Everybody would be at The Glen. Kate wouldn't want to miss that. Sam would surely bring her. Paddy described what it was like.

"Young kids running around, dogs yapping, women bringing their pies and cookies and adding to what the camp cook has ready," he talked aloud as he thought of the welcome the drive always received.

But Sam would miss the drive and Paddy had wanted to show Sam how good he was on the water. He knew he'd always been like that. The middle child crying, "Look at me! Look at me!" although he would never admit that to anyone. He'd run off at fourteen to join the war for the same reason. It was the search for excitement and attention that drew him and found him now bringing logs down the river.

"You ever ride the logs?" he was asked.

Paddy wasn't sure of the boy's name. Ansel or Antoine something. A French Canadian name, he thought. He remembered the boy was a good clog dancer evenings when the men brought out a harmonica and danced, playing cards and smoking their Bull Durhams. Paddy thought he was a pretty good dancer himself. Pretty good at most things, if he thought about it.

"Yeah, I've ridden logs. Poked the stragglers hung up shore bound. Done most all of it. Stood on slippery rocks out in the river where a log's likely to get stuck on a boulder. No high bankers for me."

"High bankers?"

"Men looking to tend an easy patch of river."

"This will be my first drive."

Paddy looked at the eager face and thought he wouldn't be so eager at day's end, sopping wet, standing by a big fire 'til he steamed dry and he could bed down. He'll find out soon enough. He wasn't a bad kid and might turn out to be a good driver if he had courage. Why sour or scare him? Just tell him what to expect.

"Don't go volunteering for every thing right away," Paddy said. "Watch and learn so you don't get hurt."

"You ever come close?"

"Lotsa times. Yeah." He thought of last spring when he volunteered to break up a jam. He'd been wanting a turn in the jam boats that followed behind the log drive and were brought to the front when needed. He had his mind set to be an oarsman, if not this year then next. A good one could earn four dollars a day.

"A key log was holding back a mass in one of the bad spots between Blue Ledge and Deer Run." Paddy recalled the problem he volunteered for. "A key log is like the keystone that supports an arch. Once the key log is dislodged, the jam collapses and disentangles. "

"What happened?"

"I reached out from the bow and hooked onto a stuck log. There's always three men in the boat, the oarsmen in the middle. The oarsman jumped out and tied up. We unlocked the mess with pikes and axes. Careful and slow like until we located the key log. A few swings. And then you listen."

"For what?"

"For shifting logs. Get out fast before it takes you under when they get moving again."

"Oh." He looked at Paddy and scratched his head. Seems like that's all he'd been doing all winter. Scratching at lice and bed bugs. They all had.

"Like I said, stick close to me and watch." If he couldn't have little brother Sam to show the ropes, this eager face looking up at him, all big eyes would do. Better find out his name though. Can't call them all Frenchy.

Ten

On an April morning when melting snow brought fouled footwear from mud-filled ruts, Jenny followed Ambrose to Miss Wickham's door. They used the cast iron boot scraper on the porch before knocking. Behind them dark clouds muddied the sky, shoved by a southwest wind that swayed tree tops. Hazel, answering their knock, stood in the open door surveying their boots with a frown before inviting them in to the front parlor.

It was a comfortable room smelling of furniture polish. The white ironstone tureen on the scarred pine table held pussy willows and forsythia that had been forced, suggesting spring had arrived inside. Inviting chairs had nearby small tables covered with books and magazines. Dust motes floated in the air and glittered with reflected daylight coming through the large front windows on either side of the tall grandfather clock. Braided rugs covered the wide boarded pine floor. The selective mix of furnishings, the prints of flowers on the wall above the child's cross-stitch sampler that a younger Grace Wickham had made years back, created a home that was comfortable and welcoming.

The grandfather clock struck the half hour just as Gracie came into the room from her back office wearing a long black skirt with a white shirtwaist; her carrot-colored thick braid twisted to a coil at the nape of her neck; both arms extended in a welcome.

"Here you are. I hoped we'd meet again. Any luck?"

Jenny shook her head.

Ambrose spoke instead. "She just arrived on the stage and wanted to see you."

"Nothing yet," Jenny answered. "But I came to see if you'd come with me to the tannery here. I went to the one in North Creek and..." She wrinkled her nose to indicate her distaste and looked to Miss Wickham with pleading eyes.

"Of course I'll go with you. You'll join us, Ambrose?"

"No, Gracie. I was just heading out the door to join Dillon. See some more of the skidways."

"Don't let us hold you then."

He turned to the door to leave. "Join me for dinner when I get back?"

They agreed, and after he left Gracie suggested they have tea before going to the tannery. A grateful Jenny joined her in the kitchen where Hazel had just taken cornbread out of the oven. A bean soup simmered on the big cook top and though Jenny had already eaten, the savory smells were enticing. She pushed away the thought of asking for just a taste in order to tell Miss Wickham of her experience in North Creek.

"It quickly disillusioned me about investigating other tanneries. But I knew you were here and I decided to try Wevertown before I gave up."

It sounded as if Jenny intended to abandon her quest if her brother wasn't in Wevertown. After she'd heard all Jenny had to say, she walked to where her outer things hung on the wooden clothes tree by the front door and suggested they set off for the tannery.

Wagons loaded with the necessary hemlock bark from nearby woods or with hides shipped up from South America rumbled along beside them as dogs chased and barked at the wagon's wheels. They saw a man coming toward them with an odd gait that caused Jenny to clutch Miss Wickham's elbow. As the man reached them Gracie said, "Morning, Charlie."

He tipped his hat. "And to you, Miz Wickham."

After he passed Gracie explained, "That's Charlie Sweeney who lost a leg in the war. Someone carved a wooden leg for him after he got back. He kicks it out in front of him as he walks which does look a bit awkward coming toward you."

When Jenny shuddered, Gracie squeezed her arm and said, "He's a good man, Jenny." She smiled and added, "He can make a racket stomping at a square dance but the ladies don't seem to mind."

They finally gave up conversation rather than shout. There was little they could do to keep the mud from their high buttoned shoes as they walked at the side of the rattling wagon road.

When they came to the tannery entrance, Gracie said, "Timothy McCarthy is the manager and a friend. He'll know if your brother's here." They paused momentarily at the open office door where Timothy was talking to another man who soon left.

Timothy had a more confident look this winter since the critical owner who'd threatened to fire him was no longer in charge. The new absentee owners of the tannery were giving the manager freedom to operate and things seemed to be going well.

Gracie introduced Jenny and told of her search. "I've been out sick for a week or so," Timothy said, "which means right now I can't put a face to that name."

Miss Wickham's raised eyebrows indicated her concern about his illness but she was here on Jenny's business, so she asked, "Would Leland have the name on his payroll?"

At the door of the bookkeeper's small office, Timothy introduced them to Leland Finley. If the bookkeeper was a color, it would be grey. Thinning grey hair, grey eyes looking over half glasses, a grey pallor. Even his dark suit was grey. The contrast with his wife, Lydia, caused people to speculate she married him for his money but Lydia, in a world of rough men, loved her husband's gentle ways and brought color into Leland's life. Lydia always looked like an exotic bird dressed in the latest fashions over her well-corseted figure. Gracie thought Lydia would love meeting Jenny, who also dressed more fashionably than the wives living in the tenancies. Lydia Finley, with her whimsical interests, the latest being the "science" of Phrenology with its head maps analyzing mental faculties, would find a kindred soul in Jenny's fashions and interest in fortune tellers and séances. Phrenology practitioners had only to measure head bumps to know a person's true self, according to Lydia. If Jenny stayed in Wevertown, Gracie was sure they'd enjoy each other's company.

Within minutes Leland Finley produced a list of workers' names. Timothy hadn't remembered the man's name but it was there on the bookkeeper's payroll. Lewis LaPierre had only recently been hired.

Jenny gasped and reached out for Miss Wickham's arm to steady herself. "He's here!" She rocked back and forth holding her arms to her chest. "I found him! Imagine! He's here!" Her exuberance brought smiles at such obvious joy.

The manager left for the floor to ask for her brother while Jenny stood on tip-toe, her eyes searching the wide opening to the work room.

In the large open room, two-dozen men were busy at a variety of tasks. Some bent over half barrels, scraping flesh from the hides, others pushed open carts with hides in various stages, several stood on the narrow wooden walkway stirring and lifting and turning hides in the vats of steaming liquor that cured the leather. Pounding, scraping, cutting, dumping, grinding bark; each was employed in a task that ended in the finished product. The stench of rotting hides ready to be processed was overwhelming and Jenny sniffed unappreciatively.

Timothy returned, shaking his head. "The men tell me he didn't come to work today. Didn't come back to the boarding house last night."

Jenny looked like someone had squeezed the air out of her. Gracie considered asking to speak to anyone out on the floor who'd last seen Jenny's brother but thought better of it. Lewis LaPierre was a young man and may have overdone celebrating his day off. That would explain his not returning to the boarding house.

Jenny made no attempt to hide her disappointment.

The bespectacled bookkeeper spoke up. "He'll probably be back. Check again tomorrow." With a rueful smile he turned back to his office. The women thanked the manager, said their goodbyes, and left.

"We can go over later and introduce you to the woman who runs the boarding house and see what she knows," Gracie said. "No point in going now when the men will be showing up for their noon meal and she's busy."

The tannery boarding house was on the same side of the road as the tannery but closer to the corner near the hotel, across the street and not far from Miss Wickham's house. The building was a two story rectangle once painted white but now mud splattered and dirty grey from the nearby traffic. It was run by Cora Collins, who brooked no nonsense from the twenty or more single men that lived there. The married men with families lived across the road beyond the Methodist church, in a cluster of small box-like houses called "the tenancies."

Outside the sun shone, but gloom filled Jenny's face as they walked past the boarding house. Gracie tried to think of something to ease Jenny's disappointment. She looked at her father's gold watch on its chain against her slim chest. "If we hurry we could catch Sam Somerville at the farm for his noon dinner," she said cheerfully. "He's recently back from Newtown Logging Camp and if you describe Lewis he might be able to tell you something."

She wanted to keep Jenny's hopes up and keep the gullible girl traveling alone out of harm's way. Her brother was on the Wevertown payroll but the manager didn't remember him among the men and now he was missing. Had he gone somewhere else?

"Just think of the good news that you've found him, Jenny. Now tell me, have you been keeping your husband informed of your whereabouts?"

Jenny's smooth skin colored and Gracie guessed the answer. It seemed there was more to Jenny than she was revealing. "You could send a telegram from the hotel with the good news that you found your brother here," she said. Jenny remained quiet as they rode on.

Later, when they pulled into the maple-lined drive of the Somerville farm, Jenny still hadn't answered Miss Wickham's question.

At the farmhouse door, Sam's mother said he'd been home but left again to haul bark. Mrs. Somerville was grey haired, a tall woman of some fifty or sixty years with little time for small talk. Like most farm wives, the hard life of producing children and the many chores expected of her took a toll, carving deep grooves on either side of her stern mouth and lined a furrowed forehead. All of it making her appear older.

There was no responding smile when Gracie said, "Just tell him we stopped by." She considered having the sick Kate meet Jenny and quickly dismissed it as not a good time. Jenny had not left the buggy but had been distracted for a short time by the ride into the countryside and that was enough for now.

Gracie thought of something else and reminded Jenny they'd be seeing Ambrose at dinner. "If he's been visiting logging camps, he might have heard something."

Eleven

It was Sam Somerville entering the hotel's dining room and coming to Miss Wickham's table that changed Jenny Crane's mood.

She'd been drumming her fingertips on the white tablecloth, moving pickle and jelly dishes around, pushing away the basket of rolls, sighing, squirming in her chair, playing with her wedding ring, and finally examining a strand of her black hair, curling it around her finger. Her eyes had been searching the room as if her behavior would remind Miss Wickham of her earlier promise to go to the boarding house to see what could be learned by talking with the men who worked with her brother. Ambrose was full of his day's adventure with the log drive superintendent, John Dillon, and happy for an audience of Jenny and Gracie.

Dillon was respected, Ambrose said, by the loggers who knew his genius for getting the logs to the big boom, that giant floating barricade that spanned the Hudson River and corralled the logs when they reached Glens Falls, ready for the sawmill.

"We went to a different dam holding back the water that keeps the logs..." He had Gracie's attention but not Jenny's as he went on and reached for the gravy boat sitting next to the large blue and white platter of fried chicken. Already on the proprietor's corner table sat a basket of grainy bread slices next to a large blue and white platter of chicken smothered with glazed onions, placed there by the waitress, Annie. Ambrose smiled at Jenny and held the gravy for Jenny to help herself. She shook her head and listlessly reached for a small chicken leg.

"Gravy, Jenny? No? Well, Dillon releases the logs furthest away first. All these brooks and ponds and lakes with crib dams." The planning that went into the log drive reminded Ambrose of the military planning from his war years. "Made of rocks and logs, you see, holding back until released by this man's plan." He paused, "Until the moment they're freed to travel along on a cushion of water."

Thinking of the drama of the log drive, Gracie said, "And when these hundreds—thousands really, of logs move along, jostling and bumping, you hear them if you're near the river." She smiled, "It can wake you in the night, the banging, the boom and bumping." But she realized Jenny wasn't listening and finished lamely, "A sound like no other."

Jenny squirmed in her chair and looked from one to the other with her troubled eyes, then turned to examine a strand of her black hair again, curling it around a finger. Gracie's velvet brown eyes studied Jenny. She didn't want to sound as if she was scolding the girl's behavior. "We'll ask at the boarding house when we finish dinner, Jenny. Just as I promised." Which was how the meal was ending when Sam Somerville walked across the dining room and stood at their table.

"Your housekeeper said you were here." Sam's words were to Miss Wickham but his eyes fastened on Jenny.

"Mother said you stopped by." His face colored and he choked on his words before he could get out "You wanted to see me?"

Sam was the youngest brother in the handsome green-eyed Somerville family. His large farmer's hands extended from his heavy woolen jacket to play with his felt hat, turning it round and round as he stood before them.

Ambrose made the introductions and Jenny sat up all smiles, interested at last in something other than crib dams and logs bumping down the Hudson, and her own strand of hair.

"Miss Wickham tells me you were at the camp where my brother, Lewis LaPierre, worked." She smiled up at him invitingly. "We think he's now here in Wevertown."

Sam sat down awkwardly in the empty chair Ambrose offered and stared at Jenny's face while she drew him out; the girl now suddenly energized. She leaned forward bringing her face close to his, opened her aquamarine eyes wide and stared into his. "You were at Newtown Loggers?" she asked.

He answered her questions mostly by nodding his head, rocking slightly back as if scorched by her radiance, her closeness and the smell of lilacs. He reached a thick finger into his shirt collar to pull it away and cool his flushed face. Gracie and Ambrose exchanged amused glances.

"But you don't remember someone named Lewis LaPierre?"

He shook his head no.

"What did you do while you worked there?"

That required more than a nod or a yes or no, and Sam began to relax as he told her of the work he did in the short time he was at the logging camp.

The waitress, Annie, hovered nearby not wanting to miss anything until she came so close that Ambrose looked up inquiringly. She blushed and said, "Need more gravy?" You could hear Ireland in her voice when she spoke. Off the boat only last fall, Annie was curious about everything in her new land, especially women's latest fashions and Jenny's traveling suit was certainly that. And now Annie looked curious about the effect Jenny was having on Sam Somerville.

Was Jenny aware of the effect she was having on Sam? Gracie wondered. His face was red and a sheen of perspiration glistened on his wide brow. She elected to intervene by suggesting it might be a good time to visit the boarding house across the road and see if Lewis was back. Ambrose declined the invitation to accompany the women to the boarding house. Sam stood and stammered something about heading back to the farm, although he made no motion to leave, his eyes following Jenny as she crossed the room.

54

Cora Collins met the two women at the boarding house entrance. She was a door-filling woman with the thick neck and shoulders of a man, her grey streaked hair pulled severely away from her face and gathered in a knot at the top of her head. She ran her boarding house with a scowling attitude and the single men who lived there generally abided by her rules.

Cora's stern face broke into a broad smile at the sight of Miss Wickham. "Well, who have you brought us?" she said after critically eyeing Jenny. The young woman introduced herself and told the story of her search for her brother.

Cora shook her head. "He's only been here a little over a week." Her voice was a scratchy growl. "Went off Saturday night with Moody Bedell to Glens Falls. Haven't seen hide nor hair of them since." She ushered them into the parlor across from the dining room. Some of the boarders were already gathered to smoke their pipes and play cards.

Gracie wondered what reason Lewis would give for not showing up for the work he'd just found. Not a very good start if he wanted to keep his job. But then she thought of his inheriting the farm and realized he wouldn't need tannery work now. But he didn't know that and his behavior did seem irresponsible.

"Here, you men," Cora said. "This is Lewis LaPierre's sister. Come looking for him."

The men looked at the women standing in the doorway and a few sat up with interest at the sight of Jenny. They didn't often see a beautiful young woman so fashionably dressed in their small hamlet unless they caught sight of Lydia Finley out walking that little white dog of hers. But Lydia only did that when the men were at work. And here was this beauty standing in their living quarters.

Gracie nodded to the ones she knew. "Any of you work with him? Anything you can tell us? When you think he might be back?"

The men exchanged looks, scowled and shook their heads. Gracie was surprised no one offered any information until a young man she knew as Phonse Roblee said, "You talkin' 'bout Frenchie?"

Jenny couldn't be surprised at the nickname. The French-Canadian children had always been called that at school.

Another man spoke up. "Don't 'spect French Lewey feel's he's gotta work for a while. Had more than his paycheck after some of us played cards with him."

Jenny blushed uncomfortably. Gracie wondered if this was something Jenny didn't know about Lewis.

The silence in the room grew until Gracie said, "If her brother returns will someone send word? Jenny's staying over at the hotel."

Heads bobbed in agreement as they scanned Jenny appreciatively one last time, and then returned to filling their pipes and picking up their cards. The women thanked Cora Collins and left.

Outside Gracie said, "You're welcome to come home with me if you don't want to sit alone in your room." But Jenny shook her head and had little more to say. The news of her brother winning at cards had evidently surprised her and her disappointment at his recent disappearance clearly showed. As they walked in the gathering darkness she reminded Miss Wickham that she hadn't seen him in three years, years when a young man was busy growing up. "He could be a very different person now."

Gracie stood in the darkening night, feeling uneasy about the way the day had gone and watched Jenny slowly walk up the steps to the large porch of the hotel and disappear inside. She shook her head, turned toward her house, and was inside before a hired buggy stopped in front of Baldoon's. The lone passenger bent in a theatrical gesture to sweep back his shoulder length hair and pull his grey woolen cape closer before stepping out; then reached up to pay the driver and turned toward the hotel entrance.

Twelve

Eddie Crane had been the spoiled, only child of a fading actress, responsible for the boy seeing a side of city life in seedy hotels. His mother's one gift to her son, other than providing a few early elocution lessons, had been reading Shakespeare aloud to him with the hope hc would take an interest in the theater.

But Eddie preferred the quicker rewards from cards he'd learned from the fatherly figures of stagehands. When his mother died from a combination of alcohol and laudanum, and with no father in sight, he was stranded in the city of Troy, New York, where they owed back rent. Her demise freed him to leave and move on to card games in whatever city he found himself, which was how he met Galvin Swagger in Saratoga. The sometime chemist recognized that with the right clothes and polish the handsome young man's stage presence and ear for Shakespeare had potential. Little Eddie Crane would take the stage in a role different than his mother imagined.

"You, my dear fellow...you will be the last ingredient for this healing brew. With the right promotion this syrup has great possibilities. And your voice will spread the good word."

Swagger laughed as he went on. "Think of it, Eddie. Swooning females will happily exchange their coins for the promise of you in a bottle. All you need is a title." While Eddie considered a royal title and whether a Duke was higher than a Count or vice versa, Swagger rasped, "No. No. A Doctor! It's only logical that a doctor knows what's best for you."

Eddie began to see himself differently as Doctor Crane. He stood taller, spoke better, dressed elegantly and convinced himself he lived to alleviate human suffering. His theatrical looks, including a mane of shoulder length brown hair, Roman nose, sensuous lips and silvery grey eyes, determined which partner would face the public. Both partners preferred to be clean-shaven in the latest fashion for men, but that was all they shared in appearances.

Swagger's tangled mass of grey-pepper hair rose around his huge head as if electrically charged, and his shuffling walk produced an image of a benign bear wearing rumpled, food stained clothes, an exterior that hid a shrewd mind. He liked the deception. Swagger was content to stay in Saratoga playing alchemist and sorcerer of the sauce while his partner went on the road.

Dr. Crane's audiences heard his silvery tones from the stage. "Health care from a bottle!" as Eddie held the bottle up with a flourish. "This syrup has brought relief to thousands! Carried health to the suffering, hope to the despondent and strength to the weak."

From the label on each amber bottle of Dr. Crane's Golden Medicine Discovery beamed the smiling face of the doctor himself, Edward Crane. At the time anyone could call himself a doctor. Though licensed doctors spoke out against abuses, patent medicine was a legal and profitable business in the 1870's. No law prohibited the partners from selling their compound.

People dissatisfied with previous treatments by their doctors, desperate, or just plain curious, could take Dr. Crane's Golden Medicine Discovery and find a remedy, an elixir, a panacea. The magic syrup was concocted from vegetable extracts with alcohol, and added to the mix were derivatives of the poppy plant which had narcotic properties.

Newspaper advertisements and posters told more than the business card Edward handed Jenny when they first met that read *Dr. Crane's Golden Medicine Discovery*. Smaller letters below that read, *Cure where other medicines fail*. He liked to believe Jenny never heard it called snake oil.

Dr. Crane's syrup kept good company. The popular Lydia Pinkham's Vegetable Compound was favored by temperance matrons who imbibed regularly for their health, unaware Pinkham's contained 15 to 20% percent alcohol.

"You're a doctor?" That afternoon in the Saratoga hotel as she looked up at him with eyes of a startling aquamarine, Jenny's breathless little girl's voice affected him. For one of the few times in his life, Eddie was speechless.

Before meeting Jenny, Edward had traveled a circuit of rural regions devoid of real doctors, promising relief for far more than an aid to digestion with his syrup. He assured his customers comfort from a variety of ailments. High blood pressure, menstrual cramps, arthritis, gastric ulcers, sprains, injuries, atherosclerosis and melancholia could all be helped.

He soon moved beyond carnivals and fairs with their kerosene pan-lamps lighting the grounds, using advance men who hit the town to spread the word. Dr. Crane would follow a week later with samples to be left in general stores and pharmacies in small hamlets and towns. Within a few years he'd moved on to the lecture halls, all engineered by his invisible partner Galvin Swagger.

Now Eddie sat alone in the mansion's parlor reading, his legs crossed carefully not to ruin his creased trousers. Under a *Hints and Happenings* column in the *Gazeteer* he read: *The Board of Supervisors on Friday last fixed the yearly salary of the County judge at $2,000 and the District Attorney at $1,000.* Eddie smiled to himself, thinking of certain gifts that would increase both official salaries and protect Morrissey's pool hall and gambling house. Although gaming houses were illegal in Saratoga, Eddie doubted the reformers would make any headway. Gambling brought economic benefits in rents, jobs and all the goods and services the gaming houses needed.

He shifted in his Morris chair and turned the page. A different item caught his eye. Maybe he should show this to Swagger. *Diplomas are not difficult to obtain from a certain college*

59

willing to qualify you and your horse if the cheque was large enough.
He hadn't considered a diploma. What would his partner think?

It was Swagger who decided Jenny would sit silently on the
stage while Dr. Crane embroidered tales of a sick woman who
once could barely walk. This was Jenny's clue to walk across
the stage at the right moment, fully recovered by ingesting the
wonderful syrup that restored her health. She was never
introduced as Edward's wife. Females in the audience were left
to fantasize about the handsome doctor. Eddie went to the
kitchen to refresh his drink.

"Oh, Dr. Crane. I didn't knows you wuz in the house."
Mrs. Armstrong stood at the sink, her arms in sudsy water.

Eddie frowned. Why did Swagger keep her on when she
irritated him with her constant jabbering? He crossed the room
to pick up the ice shaver on the counter next to the icebox.

"Oh, I'll do that for you," she started toward him, her
soapy hands spilling water on the floor.

"No, thank you," he glared to stop her. She continued
wringing her hands on a dishtowel, still beaming at him with
good humor. He couldn't stand such cheerfulness this early in
the day.

Unexpectedly she asked, "Do you know why the spring
birds is sad?"

Did she think he would answer? With her beak of a nose
she looked like a drab brown wren with the voice of a crow.
His silence didn't stop her from smiling at him and finishing her
joke.

"Because their bills are over dew! Over due, you see." She
beamed at him as if she'd just answered the teacher's question
correctly.

Eddie reached for the bottle in the cupboard and to distract
her asked, "Have you emptied the ice pan, Mrs. Armstrong?"
He looked at the bottom of the icebox where melting ice
collected.

"Air. I did. Does it first thing when I comes in in the
morning." Her cheerfulness couldn't be easily dismissed. She

shook out the towel as if she was fluffing up her wings to fly off. But no. She had more to say.

"I was tellin' Mr. Swagger bout my sister. You know the one I call a squirrel?"

Birds, squirrels? Eddie winced and gave himself a generous dose of bourbon over the ice shavings.

"Collects things, she does. That's why I call her a squirrel. Now she's got that old calendar and I keeps telling her it's no longer 1872 but she sez she likes the pitcher on it. Why doesn't she cut it off and save it if she likes it so much? Or paste it on a calendar with the right dates, I ask you?"

Eddie had no intention of answering her rhetorical question. He'd like to strong-arm Mrs. Armstrong and shut her up for good. His play on words brought a grimace to his face at his silent joke. Unfortunately their housekeeper took this as an encouraging smile.

"Keeps collecting when she doesn't have room. Where will you put it, I ask?" Mrs. Armstrong shook her head and searched his face as if it had the answer. He glared at her, wondering why Swagger found her amusing. When she wasn't blathering she was singing. With his drink in hand he returned to his Morris chair.

What was it with the Irish? NINA posters in restaurant windows didn't discourage them. Signs read *No Irish Need Apply* and they applied anyway. She was cheap enough. Molly Maguire Armstrong cost them a dollar a day with a bottle of Dr. Crane's Golden Medicine Discovery given at the end of the week. But were any of them quiet?

He settled in his chair and stared at the wall at a painting by Thomas Cole, father of the Hudson River artists. Swagger had insisted Eddie know things like that. For all he knew, it might have come with the house they rented.

Sipping his drink he studied the painting that made him think of Jenny. Where was she? Probably some fancy hotel in Lake George with a lake and mountains like the painting. He muttered to himself, "She tells me she's looking for her brother...a brother I've never met."

61

"Excuse me, sir." Mrs. Armstrong stood in the doorway.

He turned his head and gave her an icy stare. "Yes?"

"Don't like to disturb you..." She came mincing toward him like a bird looking for some crumbs and timidly held out the paper in her hand. "Must be important. It's a telegram."

Eddie tore it from her outstretched hand and dismissed her with a curt "Thank you." Jenny's telegram told him where she was in the Adirondacks. At last! The time had come for Edward to claim Jenny as his wife.

He'd leave a note for Swagger.

Thirteen

Upstairs in Baldoon's hotel, the waitress Annie held the blue silk to her face as she studied her image in the looking glass with unsmiling scrutiny.

"It will be a long time before I can afford such a dress," she muttered to herself in the quiet room. She silently compared herself to the blue silk's owner. She could see she was the same size, with the same black hair, although Annie's was tightly curly, rather than wavy, and pulled severely back from her face with tendrils always seeking to escape.

"Jenny Crane should wear green," she whispered to the mirror. "This is so right with my blue eyes."

Annie had earlier heard the owner of the blue silk leave for the boarding house with Miss Wickham to learn what she could about her brother. Still, the smell of Jenny's lilac toilet water lingered in her room.

She could hear her Guardian Angel warning her. "If you're found in a guest's room without cause, you'll be fired, missy, and you know it."

But Mr. Devilment hushed her up quickly. "I'm only looking, is all."

There it was, the imp that got her in trouble with her curiosity versus the guardian angel who brought her safely over the water to a new life. And she did love fashionable clothes. Not that the young Mrs. Crane had brought that many with her, but what was there looked quality.

It was another waitress who'd teased Annie how "curiosity killed the cat." Something Annie O'Shea would remember later. And she was teased for the voice of Ireland every time she opened her mouth. Other local families and tannery men were Irish immigrants as well, but Annie, just off the boat, had the strongest brogue. So thick it was sometimes hard to understand her when she spilled her words quickly. Her innocence about the manners and ways of her new country made her an easy target for the banter of others, and she was determined to learn quickly.

She had crossed the ocean in steerage with little more than the clothes on her back. Her mother's cousin with her cold water flat and tribe of red-nosed children had quickly directed her to the agency that sent young immigrants from the city, fanned out to where domestics were hired at cheap wages. The woman in charge, surely another Guardian Angel, must have taken a fancy to Annie, for she was fortunate to be sent to such a kind employer.

However, Annie didn't think she was so fortunate when she experienced the far below zero temperatures in her first winter in the Adirondacks. But she loved the lively atmosphere of Baldoon's Hotel (like Mr. Devilment does), the bustle of overnight guests arriving and leaving and the people who came just to dine. She watched the women who stepped off the stagecoaches and sashayed in, adjusting their bustles and beribboned bonnets, or the latest little saucer-like hats tipped to one side, like the one worn by Mrs. Crane. Jenny, Miss Wickham called her.

Annie surveyed the room she had entered that a chambermaid would be familiar with, but not a waitress. To the right of the door stood a pine clothespress where she had found the blue silk hanging. Under the dormer window a white bowl and pitcher for washing sat on a small pine cupboard with storage space below for the chamber pot. A large white iron bed dominated the room with its dark green counterpane and colorful quilts piled at the foot. A print framed by birch bark pieces hung above the bed. It was a print of one the artist painted in past summers only a short distance from the hotel. Two men paddled a canoe in swirling water of blues and greens. Her friend Agnes could have told her it was one of Winslow Homer's. Annie only knew she liked the colors and would ask about the print. But then realized her questions would reveal Mr. Devilment was in charge when she'd entered the room. She didn't want to lose her job.

Annie had been working in the hotel only a short time when Mr. Baldoon introduced his friend, that string bean of a woman with so many freckles and that orange hair. Annie's own mother had that same shade, and when she brushed Annie's black curls, thanked the saints for not passing on the cursed color. Surely that was the work of her Guardian Angel. She smiled to herself at the thought that Miss Wickham had something in common with her dear mum back in County Mayo; Mum, who first told Annie about her Guardian Angel and Mr. Devilment.

Like everyone else, Annie had warmed to Mr. Baldoon's friend, to the gentleness of this different looking woman. Annie thought Miss Wickham's best feature was the wide spaced eyes that were such velvet brown as to be almost black, beneath fringes of pale, golden lashes that were nearly invisible among the light freckles that swarmed across her face. Intelligent eyes, the woman had, under high arched brows. Surely Miss Wickham's eyes had taken in the way Sam Somerville acted when he met Jenny Crane in the dining room.

Little escaped Annie's own quick eyes. "Anyone could see Sam was struck dumb in Jenny's presence," Annie muttered to herself. "And her a married woman! Did Sam Somerville know that? Maybe he didn't care. Mrs. Crane wasn't thinking of her reputation though, was she?"

Annie knew she'd never look at another man if she was married. Harry Doyle, harness salesman who stayed at Baldoon's whenever he was in this part of his territory, had noticed her right after she was hired. Holding the dress in front of her, picturing Harry dancing with her, she swayed lightly back and forth before the mirror. She knew she was pretty.

Didn't Harry tell her? Responsible about his job, too. She was sure Harry's intentions were honorable. Mr. Baldoon liked him, she could see that. Of course, Mr. Baldoon liked everybody. But her Guardian Angel whispered just then, "He won't like it if he finds you in this room."

She reluctantly returned the dress to the clothes press from where she'd taken it, patted her hair as she turned again to the looking glass. She opened the door quietly to check no one was in the hall. Believing she was unseen, she slipped noiselessly down the main stairs just in time to hear loud voices. What was going on?

At the bottom of the wide staircase, the owner of the blue dress was being held roughly on the arm by an elegantly dressed man with a mane of silky, brown hair. They stood near the bottom step where he appeared to be trying to lead her away up the stairs. Sam Somerville stood nearby, looking as if he wanted to say something but hesitated to interfere.

"We were just talking!" The young woman raised her voice as she tried to tear her arm away. "Sam was telling me about the camp Lewis was in."

"Jenny, keep your voice down." The man held her arm so tightly he wrinkled the sleeve of her jacket. "We can't talk here."

Annie had left the bedroom just in time. (Thank you, Guardian Angel.) Was this handsome man her husband? It must be from the way Sam looked guilty and the way the man was trying to get her up the stairs. What had been said that she'd missed? Had the husband, if it was her husband, arrived just now and caused a scene? Oh, that would have been something to see. Maybe if Agnes had been in the dining room she could tell her. But their voices were getting louder. He said something about Jenny's proper place was with him. Yes, he had to be the husband.

At that moment she saw Jenny Crane whirl away from the grip the man had on her arm and march toward the front door. Sam Somerville stood there like a statue and then turned around to go out the front door as well. After Jenny? Did the husband see that? Would he follow for more arguing outside? She watched the husband draw himself up and go to the front desk. Annie shrunk against the wall in a clumsy attempt to become invisible and moments later saw the man stride up the wide main staircase with the key in his hand.

This was the most excitement she'd seen since she started working in the hotel. It was like one of those plays Harry promised to take her to see at the Glens Falls Opera House.

Where was Mr. Baldoon? He wouldn't have approved of the way the husband grabbed his wife like that. Well, she brought it on herself, flirting with Sam in such a way. What was Jenny Crane doing traipsing around the countryside? Leaving her husband and saying she was trying to find her brother?

The lobby was quiet again as Annie looked around and saw nobody was looking at her. She started for the dining room to see what further details her friend Agnes could give her.

Fourteen

Baldoon's Hotel stirred at winter's end with arriving drummers ready to travel the work week on business. Like early robins, salesmen came with their samples, anxious to get ahead of the competition.

Elsewhere in the hotel, the desk clerk who gave Dr. Crane the key to his wife's room knocked on the door to Ambrose's office and told him what had transpired.

"He presented his card, Mr. Baldoon, and the room was registered to his wife. I didn't feel I could say no." Let someone else tell the proprietor about the scene Annie had described to him. The desk clerk was a small, fussy man with pale, receding hair that he carefully combed over his forehead to one side. Reuben Sawyer had worked at the hotel before Mr. Baldoon bought it and he'd been kept on.

Unaware of any disturbance when he showed the new guest to his wife's room, Reuben had given key to the husband without question. He should have known it would be all right but he wanted to keep this job. To his employer he said, "And the man who said he was Jenny's husband was a doctor. His card said so, and he was distinguished looking and wearing expensive clothes. And well spoken, too."

Reuben knew his employer did not discriminate against Jews as many of the hotels did, but he needed to assure Mr. Baldoon he had given a key to a respectable person. Everyone knew what the advertisements meant when you read things like

Gentile trade solicited or *Guests will enjoy our Christian library.* Some even saying *No Hebrew patronage solicited.* No, Baldoon's Hotel never advertised in that manner, and his employer let that Jewish peddler use the barn when he passed through. Even bought him a drink.

But that new waitress, Annie something, came hurrying up to tell him there had been some kind of harsh words and the wife had stormed out.

"It's all right, Reuben. I'll have a word with him," his employer said. The two men walked back to the lobby.

Reuben was relieved. "Thank you, Mr. Baldoon." He began busying himself lining up room keys in each of the boxes behind the desk, pleased it appeared no more was to be said. From the corner of his eye, he watched Mr. Baldoon climb the stairs. It looked as if the proprietor was going to have that word with Dr. Crane now.

Reuben knew something of his employer's history. He'd learned Ambrose Baldoon's wartime experience as a Union supply officer near the end of the war enabled him to deal easily with what was involved in a business, and after searching for property had bought the old hotel four years ago. Reuben heard money came from his family's business in Massachusetts and thrifty Scottish ancestors, and not from the graft and corruption during the war that in Mr. Baldoon's military position he was required to expose. Much of the proprietor's time at the hotel was spent with suppliers, stagecoach schedules, hiring and supervising the staff; and his decisiveness and intelligence had led to greater business. But Reuben could see Mr. Baldoon's personal warmth and good cheer was the key to his success.

Everyone said Ambrose Baldoon looked like General Washington without the serious look seen in Gilbert Stuart paintings, and of course Washington wasn't bald like Mr. Baldoon. But Reuben's employer was so much taller than the average man and, weighing well over two hundred pounds, made an imposing figure. His light brows sat over clear, bright blue eyes, eyes which reportedly neither missed little nor gave it away.

Upstairs a few minutes later, Ambrose knocked on the guest room door. "Dr. Crane," he called out as he rapped lightly.

The man who stood before him in the open doorway was not as tall as Ambrose and noticeably slimmer. The hotel owner introduced himself and said he was sorry he had not met him earlier, but was acquainted with his wife.

"Ah yes, my wife." The promoter of Dr. Crane's Golden Medicine Discovery held himself in an erect pose like an actor on a stage and raised a slender right forefinger to his eyebrow, calling attention to his unusual silver grey eyes. It was as if the man thought ahead of how he would present himself, mused Ambrose.

"Then you are aware of her reason for being in these mountains?" he asked Ambrose.

"Yes, she told me. She was with us at dinner earlier this evening."

Ambrose took in the cut of the good grey suit that further accentuated the man's icy eyes. Ambrose liked good clothes himself. His own dress was immaculate, with fine dark suits, starched shirt collars and a gold watch and chain worn draped across his vest. Vests were his one vanity, with a closet holding vests of different colors and fabrics, silks, velvets and brocades. A vanity acquired after years in uniform.

Ambrose continued, "We learned the brother she's been looking for has found work here at the tannery. Although at the moment it appears he's gone off somewhere."

"As has my wife, it seems."

Ambrose smiled reassuringly. "There's not a great deal to see at this time of night. She may be back soon."

"She deserves a good spanking." As soon as the words were out of his mouth, Eddie Crane regretted them. He was facing penetrating blue eyes. His own eyes darted around the room as if he was searching for answers. How much did the man know? What else had Jenny revealed? Said about him?

Had this man heard of the scene in the lobby? Jenny's refusal to come upstairs with him?

Maybe he shouldn't have come. Jenny would have eventually returned on her own. But Swagger had insisted they needed her for the lecture in Rochester and afraid she wouldn't be back in time. Edward believed she really was looking for her brother. Told himself he hadn't been too firm with her. In spite of that scene downstairs, it was inconceivable she would leave him. Hadn't they offered her a life beyond her wildest dreams? A life far different from that farm she came from? Travel across the country as the audiences grew larger and the demand for their wonderful balm increased and brought riches Jenny never would have had without marriage to him? She could only be grateful.

"Spanking? I'm sure that won't be necessary." Ambrose's smile was tight as he studied him, guessing Jenny's husband was a good twenty years older than his wife and probably did see his wife as a disobedient child.

He took another tack. "My desk clerk showed me the calling card you gave him. You're a doctor of sorts?"

"I'm in the healing business, yes." Edward absently adjusted his floppy silk cravat, happy to change the subject. "My partner and I have a firm in Saratoga which is where I met my wife."

"And that business is?"

"Dr. Crane's Golden Medical Discovery." He had a sense this man would never be a customer and decided against further embellishment. "For a variety of ailments," he added

"I see." Ambrose thought there was falsity about the man, although he admitted he had the look many women found attractive.

Edward cleared his throat. "I've found my wife and she's found her brother. At least that's what her telegram said. "His stage voice back once more, he added, "All's well that ends well, you could say."

"Indeed," said Ambrose. "At least she knows her brother's here." He had originally intended to invite Jenny's husband

71

downstairs for a drink, learn more about the man, but now he thought better of it. Ambrose knew himself to be a good judge of men and believed there was something about Dr. Edward Crane that didn't sit right. He didn't issue the intended invitation and wished him a good night, deciding instead that he'd go see Gracie. He was sure she'd be interested in hearing that Jenny's husband had arrived.

Fifteen

Sam Somerville's wagon was still outside the hotel. The horse was tied to the post rail waiting for his owner, but Sam was nowhere in sight. The work at the tannery had long ceased and with it the noisy sounds of the day. Had Sam walked the short distance to Gracie's house for some reason? People always seemed to need to talk to Miss Wickham.

Ambrose thought about what it was that drew him to Gracie. His dead wife, Arabella, had been called a beauty and forever surrounded by admirers, but Ambrose realized that while that kind of beauty might attract many men, it didn't wear well.

Arabella had been dark haired with pale, ivory skin that never saw the sun. Petite, cloying, stormy and temperamental. What with Arabella's poor health there'd been no children. Like other families divided by the war, when he enlisted with the Union, she returned to where her loyalties were, in the South. Just before the attack on Fort Sumter, Arabella arrived safely, only to succumb to yellow fever.

Ambrose could never remember Gracie having a sick day, or the vapors, whatever they were. Grace Wickham radiated good health. Good judgment and common sense, too.

The contrast with his wife was stark. Gracie would never be considered a fashionable beauty, but he found her enlivening; her unusual coloring and features attractive; her turn of mind invigorating. There was her warmth and kindness that drew people. He strode on to her house smiling, as he acknowledged to himself it drew him to her door.

Inside the parlor the grandfather clock struck nine as Hazel answered and went to tell her employer that Mr. Baldoon was waiting. There was no sign of Sam Somerville.

When Ambrose saw that she had come from the back of the house where her office was, he said, "Hope I'm not taking you away from anything, Gracie."

"Nothing that can't wait, Ambrose. I wasn't seeing a patient." It didn't surprise her to see him again after she and Jenny had left for the boarding house. She felt equally free to stop at the hotel when she wanted to talk things over.

"Tea?" and without waiting for his answer, she started for the kitchen with Ambrose following as if that was the reason for his stopping by. Unspoken was the invitation to apple pie that would be offered with tea.

Of all the rooms in the comfortable house, Ambrose preferred the large kitchen. It seemed to be the heart of the house with its Buddha-like black cooking stove still glowing brightly. The bread ready to be baked in the morning was resting on an upper shelf to rise; bunches of yarrow and sage and other herbs he couldn't identify hung from a rough-hewn rafter above the stone sink. The marmalade cat slept in the rocking chair beside the pie cupboard; the scene orderly, warm and reassuring, which fit his image of Gracie.

A number of tea caddies sat on a shelf next to the stove. Over time he learned the caddies represented family heirlooms, gifts, or exchanges from a patient for Miss Wickham's medical treatments and her herbal medicines. Antique inlaid wooden boxes with brass handles and keyholes that may have once locked out suspected servants or greedy drinkers from the once expensive tea lined the shelf. Included in the collection were tea caddies of different colored and cut glasses, woods, tortoise shells or porcelains, all air tight to seal the essence.

And there was a choice of tea. Tonight she chose chamomile but Ambrose knew she made other healing teas from fresh herbs in the spring and dried herbs in the fall— bergamot, elderflower, ginger, hop, horsetail, juniper berry, lovage, marigold, peppermint, rosehip, thyme or valerian. Not that he knew all the different kinds but Gracie could easily list the names and properties of each of her herbal teas.

She came to the round table and reached for a chair to indicate Ambrose should join her. From the pie cupboard she took out the pie, cut a generous piece and placed it on a blue and white plate before him. Ambrose was partial to Hazel's apple pie. Around them the soft glow of the lamp light shone on the wooden floor and scatter rugs like a moonlight's shaft of ribbon.

He sat watching her. "I don't know if you've heard," he began. "Jenny's husband is here."

Gracie turned from the stove where she'd placed the kettle and smiled, revealing straight white teeth. "Really? You've seen him?"

"Reuben Sawyer gave her husband the room key after he presented his card and identified himself." He swiped at a crumb that fell on his vest.

"Jenny wasn't there?"

"I was told later there was a scene when the husband wanted her to go upstairs with him and she marched out of the hotel instead."

Gracie's high eyebrows arched even further. "What kind of a scene? You didn't see it?"

"Not when it happened. Apparently he saw her talking in the dining room with Sam Somerville."

"And that caused some distress?"

"I'm just repeating what others said, Gracie."

"I thought Sam was returning home when Jenny and I left you after dinner."

"Well, it looks like he didn't. His wagon is tied up outside the hotel."

"Still?"

75

"No sign of him though."

Gracie considered that unusual behavior for someone she believed to be a sensible young man. Instead she asked, "What's Jenny's husband like?" She remembered a man seeing Jenny off at the train station. Was it her husband? "Did he say why he's here?"

"I didn't ask." Ambrose paused and went on. "What's he like? Well, he promotes Dr. Crane's Golden Medicine Discovery." Ambrose enjoyed watching her face as each revelation brought a change to her features.

"Patent medicine?" She wrinkled her freckled nose in dismay. "He's not a real doctor then?"

"Not even half as much as you are, I suspect."

Ambrose had gradually learned the history of Grace Wickham's year at Syracuse Medical College where she was one of three female students in 1872, the year it opened. Gracie told him she'd been happy there despite the resentment of some of the men students toward the women, and would have stayed if her father's illness hadn't brought her home.

"I respect those who earn a medical license and the right to be called doctor. If I'd finished the three years of medical..." She paused, smiled at him and added, "For now Miss Wickham will do."

She knew from that one year in Syracuse and the years of assisting her father that she was capable of diagnosing symptoms, could set broken bones, lance a boil, and deliver babies if needed. But she continued to emphasize preventive medicine and using healing herbs for illnesses. When she felt it was warranted, she referred people to Dr. Martin in North Creek or to specialists in Glens Falls.

She sat opposite Ambrose thinking over what he'd told her about Edward Crane. "That explains Jenny saying her husband travels a good deal."

"He's a good deal older than Jenny. I guess some would call him urbane. Theatrical enough to be in the business of snake oil."

"And the brother? Any more word on him?"

"No."

Ambrose picked up the cup she poured for him and blew on it. "I'm sure it will be a shock to be told his sister is here looking for him."

"And Jenny is off somewhere?"

"I don't know where. Maybe somewhere with Sam."

"I wouldn't think so." In the space of a few minutes she learned Jenny's husband was here and Sam hadn't returned to the farm as he intended. Unlike him. And his reaction to Jenny at the dinner table, what was that all about? She refused to put into words an illusory sense of unease that had settled in the room with the news Ambrose brought her. She realized she'd interrupted him and asked for a further description of Jenny's husband.

"I'll be interested in your impression, Gracie. I confess to taking a dislike to the man, although I sense women might feel differently."

She smiled at the remark and said, "I usually agree with you about people. What didn't you like beside the fact he sells patent medicine?"

Ambrose hesitated for only a moment before he repeated the short conversation they'd had in Jenny's room where her husband suggested his wife needed a good spanking.

"A spanking?" she frowned, and then thought of her friend Susan and her fight for women's rights and sighed. "Unfortunately that's a common attitude. That a husband has a right to inflict physical punishment on his property and that his wife is his property." Ambrose agreed with her on women's rights and she believed he respected her independent thinking.

Ambrose had tactfully raised the question of her financial security when her father died. It was a reason many women sought marriage, but she'd told him she had income from interest on a loan her father had made. Her part time work as a correspondent for the Warrensburg paper couldn't pay much, but the barter system patients used for her services added to her income and kept her comfortable.

Ambrose held his own thoughts. He rose to go after he said he'd look for Sam if the wagon was still tied up at the hotel rail. "I'm sure there's a good reason he hasn't left," he assured her and wished her a pleasant good night.

It would be anything but.

Sixteen

It was a little before nine when the boarding house quieted on Monday evening and men in the house parlor began tamping their pipes to prepare for bed, closing checker boards, folding their cards and putting stereoscopic slides away. The unspoken signal came from the handyman, George, who came in to check the woodstove for the night. Cora Collins was in the kitchen talking to the cook who was readying breakfast supplies for the next day when Lewis LaPierre came through the back door.

"Look who the cat dragged in," Cora exclaimed in her scratchy voice. "Where have you been?" She crossed her large bosom with her equally large arms and man sized hands over the long, dark grey dress she wore, her fat legs showing thick black stockings above her black boots. "You look awful."

Lewis LaPierre was slightly taller than average height, with simian arms, a muscle-braided build, and dark, wavy hair like Jenny Crane. If asked, the boarding house matron would have said the sister had gotten all the looks. Where Jenny's skin was smooth, the brother's swarthy surface was coarse, and now emphasized with the black stubble of a beard on his face. His dark eyebrows made black commas over piercing black eyes, but his face softened when he smiled, showing a dimple and straight white teeth with some missing in the bottom.

"Do you know your sister's been here looking for you?"

He stumbled and caught himself against the wooden counter by the sink. "Really!" His dark eyes darted around the room. "Where is she?"

"At the hotel. And anxious to find you, but the condition you're in will give her a shock. You look like you slept in your clothes."

He frowned and said, "I did."

"You haven't said where you've been, got everyone wondering."

"Jail."

"What? What for?"

Cora saw the devilment in his eyes before he said, "Disturbing the peace. Saturday night in Glens Falls." And then as if he'd explained enough he asked, "Moody show up yet?"

Cora shook her head in disgust. "Not yet. And you better clean yourself up if your sister comes around again. Although she probably won't this late."

"Any chance there's something to eat?" He reached for a pickle from the glass dish sitting on the counter.

Cora swatted his hand ineffectively and said to the cook, "Heat up some of the stew we had tonight." And then with some irritation at the cook, "Never mind making a face. I'm doing it for his sister."

Her reputation for strictness and brooking no nonsense might be threatened if she showed any deviation from the rules, but the boy was back and his pretty sister would be glad, so she told herself she'd make this one exception. Not that the brother wasn't a charmer.

Upstairs in the room they shared, Phonse Roblee later listened to French Lewey's tale of a wild Saturday night with Moody Bedell. How they'd become separated and what a Glens Falls jail was like, which was an experience Phonse said he could skip. With his unremarkable features of faded brown eyes in a doughy face, Phonse watched his roommate pace the room and

80

mumble about what bad timing his sister's visit was. "Just back from jail and all."

Phonse interrupted to tell him, "I thought she was awful pretty. She came looking for you. Said she hadn't seen you in three years."

Phonse watched his roommate continue to pace the room and added, "Why don't you go over to the hotel before it gets any later and tell her you're back?"

"I'm a mess. Don't wanna scare her, Phonse. Gotta clean myself up." He shook his head as he went over what happened.

"Walked most of the thirty miles from Glens Falls, slipping in muddy ruts and being passed by wagons that splattered wet snow and mud rather than stop and give me a lift. This surprise isn't helping me think. My sister? Oh, God! Why now?" Frenchy's eyes scanned the room as if an answer could be found on the pine walls.

"Phonse, you gotta do this for me. Tell her I'll meet her in a while." He smiled appealingly and waited. It might be all right to meet her in the dark. Hadn't Phonse just said she hadn't seen him in three years?

"Don't know why you can't go over yourself once you clean up."

"You're not thinking, Phonse. This way she gets used to the idea I'm back and I don't just barge in on her. How'd she find me anyway?"

"Your letter telling her you was gonna leave the loggin' camp and look for work at a tannery. Least ways that's what she and Miss Wickham was saying when they came here earlier."

"Who's Miss Wickham?"

"Lives in that big white house across the street, near the hotel."

"Oh, her." He'd seen her around. "The black cape and hat? The woman who looks like a witch?" He laughed. "All she needs is a broom."

"Frenchy! Don't say that. Everybody likes her," Phonse protested. "Father was the doctor people went to for years. She met your sister on the train from Saratoga and she's just being nice."

Frenchy pulled his shirt over his head and muttered, "Yeah, yeah. Enough. Do this for me. Just go." He frowned to hurry Phonse along and said, "Now."

Phonse Roblee was a simple young man, one of many who worked at the tannery only too glad to have a job, with long hours six days a week. He earned a paycheck, had a roof over his head and hearty food with it, and considered himself fortunate. He had no plans for the future and expected someday to be married, although he had no idea how that would come about.

"I'm going. I'm going," and he pulled on a jacket to go to the hotel with the message for Jenny. He'd tell her that her brother needed time to get presentable and would meet her in front of the boarding house in half an hour. Why did he let himself get talked into things by that slick Frenchy?

Outside the April night had turned mild, promising winter's end. Phonse walked slowly from the boardinghouse to the hotel on the corner, unhappy with being talked into his errand. Frenchy was like that, talking fast and getting his way. Phonse chewed on the thought. Look how he'd gone off with Moody who used to be Phonse's friend. Didn't seem worried what happened to him either.

The hotel owner had been pointed out to Phonse at one time, so he knew it was Ambrose Baldoon standing behind the front desk speaking with a man who was putting a key in one of the pigeonholes that lined the board against the wall. Phonse stepped up to the desk to ask for Jenny Crane.

"Good evening." The proprietor greeted him warmly as if he was a guest checking in, which Phonse thought was real nice of the man since obviously, standing there in his work clothes, Phonse wasn't. He explained he was looking for Lewis LaPierre's sister to tell her that her brother was back.

"Well! She'll be glad to hear that." Mr. Baldoon's strong voice was full of enthusiasm. "You brought good news, young man. I'll tell her."

He liked the way the big proprietor smiled and talked to him in a hearty way as if Phonse was responsible for the news that would make the sister happy. He'd never come to Baldoon's to drink, feeling more at home in the basement tavern where the tannery workers spent their money. But he might just get himself cleaned up one of these nights and step up to the hotel bar where he now believed he'd be welcome.

Phonse walked back to the boarding house feeling better. He'd brought good news and been treated fairly. He'd have told Frenchy that, but he didn't see him in the house and wasn't about to go looking. Just back and off somewhere again...well his sister will be looking for him and he'd better show up.

He readied for bed, wondering if Moody Bedell would also show tonight. He'd have to give back the pillow he'd taken from his bed. Still, if Moody stumbled in later he wouldn't know the difference right away. Served him right if he'd spent the night in jail, too. Going off with Frenchy with the money from playing cards, when Phonse and Moody used to be such good friends. That is until French Lewey became the third roommate.

Seventeen

A mild April evening meant better days lay ahead. Skies were clear and moonlight shone down on the little hamlet. It was late for children, who should be in bed at this hour. Some diners in the hotel were heading there as well, except for men at the bar reluctant to go home who stayed for another drink. Why go home, especially if you'd rather be anywhere but there?

The pounding at the door meant someone needed her. Gracie lifted her father's gold watch where it sat on the night table. A moon, only days after being full, showed by window's light the time to be a little after three in the morning. Who would be needing help at this hour? Hazel would know. Deciding it must be an emergency, Gracie reached for her dressing gown and lit a kerosene lantern before going downstairs to open the front door.

"Moody? Is that you? Something wrong?" She held the lantern close to his face.

Moody Bedell lived at the tannery boarding house and had come at one time to see her about an infected toe. He looked wretched, shivering in the cold.

He spoke with difficulty as if it hurt to speak, his words making puffs of steam in the night air. "Better come, Miss Wickham. There's some woman on the ground."

"Who is it?"

"Never saw her before."

"Give me a minute to get dressed and I'll go with you."

Moody Bedell's name came from his mother's family and had nothing to do with his temperament, which was usually cheerful. But not tonight. He was big boned with wild reddish hair and a face of freckles now caked with dirt. His hairy wrists extended beyond the cuffs of a too-short jacket that was rumpled and dirty, and his ragged pants were too short for his tall frame. He looked exhausted.

Back and dressed for outdoors, Miss Wickham handed him the hanging lantern so he could light the way as she followed. The moon hung suspended over Mill Mountain's spiky pines, silhouetted like military spears protecting the sleepy hamlet.

They came to the side of the boarding house where a muddy path led to the privy.

"Purt near stumbled on her in the dark," Moody said.

"You didn't see anyone else?"

"No." He held the lantern in one hand and kept running the other through his hair, clearly upset over his discovery. "There. There she is."

Gracie came to where he stood and even before she looked at the face recognized Jenny Crane's burgundy traveling suit. She scanned the ground for what it might reveal but there was no evidence Jenny had been dragged there. The path was crisscrossed with images of boot prints mingled with patches of snow and mud, making it impossible to identify any one set of prints. With a sense of dread, she bent down feeling for a pulse in the carotid artery, pulled the jacket collar away from her neck, and saw the bruises.

"Is she alive?" Moody asked as his voice trembled. "Passed out, or what?"

Gracie considered her answer. "I need to look at her in my office." It was too late to harm Jenny's body further by moving her. She knew the girl was dead.

Walking back to the big white house with Jenny in his arms like a sack of grain on his shoulder, he explained how he'd stumbled upon her. He told of a wild time in Glens Falls with Frenchy. How they got separated and how he'd walked around the city looking for his friend, then stacked some wood for a family whose widowed mother paid him with a meal before he set out on the road for Wevertown. And just now back, he found the girl lying on the ground. His labored words appeared to come from fatigue rather than the weight of Jenny's small body.

The housekeeper, awakened by Moody's pounding on the door, was waiting in the parlor in her old plaid bathrobe, her white braids down at her shoulders as she silently watched Moody carry Jenny to the back room.

"Keep Margaret out of the office, will you, Hazel?" Gracie nodded to Moody to go on back to the office and spoke again to her housekeeper. "As soon as you're dressed I have an errand for you."

Moody gently lowered Jenny on to the examining table. His exhaustion appeared to dampen any further questions, and having passed his unexpected problem on to Miss Wickham, said he just wanted to leave and get what rest he could.

Hazel saw him out and came back to the office to say Cousin Margaret was sleeping soundly. "Snoring, in fact."

"I'll give you a note for a rider to take to Dr. Martin in North Creek. I'll need him tonight," she told Hazel who glanced at the girl lying on the table but said nothing.

Without questioning or commenting, **Hazel** waited for the note to be written and set off for the livery stable to send word to the coroner.

While Gracie waited for Dr. Martin, she looked at the purple bruises on Jenny's neck. Someone with strong hands had done this. Medically speaking, it looked simple enough—manual strangulation with distinct impressions of bruising on either side of her neck with no scratches. During her year at Syracuse Medical School, dead bodies were looked at dispassionately in anatomy class, although she would always have the memory of the male students who tested her with a prank.

86

The anatomy room grew unusually quiet as she raised her scalpel to make an incision on her cadaver's bladder. With the first cut, billows of smoke surrounded her. The men in her class elbowed each other and grinned with the success of their late night efforts. A few of "the boys" had spent the previous evening filling her cadaver's bladder with pipe smoke, secured it with sutures, ready for the prick of her knife.

Gracie gave them a shake of her head like a schoolmarm before giving in to the laughter that broke all around her. Of course their unsmiling professor reprimanded all with a stern lecture, but she knew she'd passed some kind of a test. After that her male colleagues left off the snide remarks on how "the female brain is not suited for science."

Now Gracie looked down at the body before her. The cadaver in anatomy class had been dried bones and wizened remains, but this girl had been full of life just hours ago. She had watched Jenny start up the steps to the hotel believing she was safe for the night. Why had Jenny gone outside again?

Gracie had said, "You're welcome to come in if you don't want to sit alone in your room." Jenny hadn't answered outright and simply shook her head no. But Ambrose said Jenny had later argued with her husband and stormed out of the hotel. He'd heard it second hand but that meant she'd gone out into the night after seeing her husband. Had the husband followed? But Ambrose talked with him in Jenny's room so it looks as if he didn't. So who did?

Print impressions under Jenny's jaw seemed to indicate she had been attacked from the front. Strong force must have been used in what she guessed was an impulsive act, with sudden death occurring by vagal inhibition when the vagas nerve was traumatized. With a bright moon Jenny would have seen who approached, wouldn't she? Was she surprised or did she know her assailant?

How long had Jenny lain there? What time had she been killed? Rigor mortis would soon set in and be fully established after twelve hours to give some indication of when she died. It may have been an impulsive act but what was the motive?

Would someone have done this if Jenny had repulsed his advances? Her clothes weren't torn or in disarray which would have indicated a struggle. What did that say about her assailant?

Her husband was staying at the hotel and would have to be told. How would he take it? Jenny hadn't indicated she was expecting him. Had he come intending to take her home? Ambrose said Jenny had stormed out of the hotel after words were exchanged in the lobby with the husband. How soon after that was she attacked?

And her brother would have to be told what happened when he returned as well. What a shock for him. She'd come looking for him, and as far as anyone knew she never got to meet him.

Eighteen

Across from the dark Wevertown tannery building, the tenancy houses were stirring with babies crying and parents rousing to the waking sounds. In the Wickham's house, the two friends looked across the office desk at each other and sighed. A young person's death always seemed an aberration, even to the medical community.

The white-haired coroner was a spare, short man with bright blue eyes and a sharp intelligence. Dr. Martin had been a family friend for years, someone Gracie had known since she was a young girl.

"The fading bruises on her arms and legs occurred some time back, Gracie," he'd said when he drew the sheet over the body. He was used to being called out at all hours but his years were showing tonight. Finished with his examination, he'd taken the big seat behind the office desk and slumped back.

"I agree." Gracie sat across from him. She steepled her fingers under her chin and said, "Makes me wonder about the husband she left. Jenny had given no indication of such abuse." Gracie looked out the big back window and saw the day brightening. It looked to be a sunny, unusually mild day for early April. Soon the first wagons would be rumbling on the road out front.

"What do you know about him?"

She slowly rolled her head in a circle to relieve her tiredness, sat up taller and said, "She didn't tell me much. I know his name, Edward Crane, and she said that he travels. It was her search for the brother's whereabouts that she mainly spoke of. Now I wonder if there was more to her leaving home."

"Getting away from a cruel marriage, you're saying?"

"Not easy for a woman, Dr. Martin. Remember Abby McFarland's story? She divorced a drunken and abusive husband and he turned around and killed the new husband."

"And was acquitted. I remember hearing of that."

"Yes. An insanity plea. But then was given custody of Abby's son. I remember the outrage of Susan's and Elizabeth's protests."

Mentioning her friend Susan Anthony usually raised men's hackles, but Dr. Martin gave no notice. The motherly Elizabeth Cady Stanton stayed home to organize and write on behalf of the cause both women championed, but Susan as the voice bore the brunt of criticism with scathing editorials and mocking cartoons.

"You think running away was what this young woman was doing to escape an abusive marriage?" Dr. Martin brought them back to the body in the room.

Gracie shook her head. "No. I'm not saying that because I don't know. But these bruises are not new and don't seem to be connected to the bruises where she was strangled. You agree?"

"Bruises that could have come from someone else, including a rough husband."

"Ambrose came over last night to tell me the husband had arrived at the hotel looking for his wife. We'll have to tell him what happened."

Dr. Martin studied her and said, "Unless he already knows."

"Even if he was abusive, it doesn't mean he killed her."

"Anyone else you can think of?"

She had seen Sam Somerville's fascination with Jenny and it bothered her that Ambrose saw his wagon last night still outside the hotel. She'd expected Sam was heading home when they parted. It wasn't something she intended to mention immediately to the coroner but it made her wonder. She disliked thinking this way.

Instead she said, "Maybe Jenny resisted someone's advances. She was out there alone at night and who knows who she ran into." Was it a self-inflicted tragedy? Walking about in a strange place after dark? It was possible to imagine Jenny standing in her burgundy suit in the dark night meeting her killer, her eyes wide with surprise.

Dr. Martin gave a skeptical look, locked his hands behind his head, thinking. His long silence caused Gracie to decide to mention what Ambrose told about the husband promoting patent medicine. She expected he would approve of it no more than she did.

"I suppose you should know the husband promotes something called Dr. Crane's Golden Medicine Discovery."

"Snake oil?"

She smiled. "The card he presented to the hotel clerk didn't say snake oil."

"Nonetheless, it bears looking into. Quacks! Phony medicine. Charlatans! That's what they are! Deceiving people with promises of miraculous cures." Dr. Martin's peppery indignation went on. "And this is the man who bruised his wife?"

"We only suspect that," she injected but he chose not to hear her.

"I know your feelings about mistreatment of women, Gracie. And tricking people with impossible promises. Bunkum and hokum! This man should be stopped!" The coroner could be excitable when he felt strongly.

She nodded and considered another problem. "You'll inform the constable of this death?" She knew he'd have to be brought in at some point regardless of her personal dislike of the man. It offended her sense of fairness to think how he would handle matters.

Dr. Martin knew her feelings about the town constable and said with some satisfaction, "Jeremiah Russell is away in Utica. Another family funeral." His mood became sanguine as he smiled and added, "Looks like this is one you'll have to solve without the good constable."

She took note of his conspiratorial grin and smiled in return, knowing she wanted to find answers herself, but said, "You're the one asking me, remember?" With some satisfaction she raised her eyebrows and turned what she said next into a question. "But perhaps before Jeremiah returns we can find some answers?"

Like two conspirators he nodded in agreement. "You do that, Gracie."

Cora was waiting when Lewis LaPierre came down to breakfast. Just before daybreak Cora had looked out her bedroom window and saw the coroner's buggy outside Miss Wickham's house. To have the doctor there and recall that Moody had come in and said he found a woman unconscious in the yard made her wonder if something might have happened to the sister. No one would ever accuse Cora of being tactful or of a sensitive nature. Besides, she liked baiting Frenchy as the newest of her boarders. She'd been too nice letting him eat after he'd missed the regular mealtime last night.

"That sister of yours comes looking for you and now she's probably gone and got herself in some kind of trouble."

Startled, he raised his voice. "What? What are you talking about?" He scowled and stepped aside her wide frame in the doorway and toward the dining room. The men were gathered around the long table having a breakfast of oatmeal, eggs, ham slices and biscuits. Large ironstone pitchers of milk stood in the middle of the table.

Cora followed him. "Coroner's over at Miss Wickham's. Did you see your sister last night?"

Phonse Roblee heard the last question and looked up from the table, interested to hear what his roommate had to say. He'd fallen asleep before Frenchy had come back in.

The brother walked over to the windows facing the tannery down the road, now eerily quiet without the noisy wagons that would show up later bringing hemlock and hides. Someone's dog was sniffing along the roadside and then bounded down into the ditch to chase what he'd discovered.

To the boardinghouse matron waiting for his answer he grumbled, "I waited outside and she never came."

"Harrumph," Cora turned toward the kitchen, determined to find out why the coroner was at Miss Wickham's. "We'll see," she muttered at the doorway to no one in particular.

In the dining room Lewis found an empty space on the bench and poured himself coffee from the speckled enamel pitcher, tipping open its attached cover, then blew on his matching cup. The man across the table looked up and exclaimed, "Frenchy! Where was you and Moody, anyway?"

"Didn't Moody tell you?" Frenchy looked around the table for his friend just as Moody came through the doorway and stood yawning, looking not in any better shape than when he returned.

But Moody had heard the question and disgustedly said, "Jail."

Spoons stopped midway to mouths. Hands stopped just short of picking up biscuits and several who hadn't heard the news before said in unison, "Jail!"

Frenchy grinned at their reaction, showing his white teeth and giving an impish look to his stubbled face. To the buzz of questions that all came to mean "why?" he looked at Moody and said, "Disturbing the peace, wasn't we, Moody?"

"Whose peace?" asked the heavy man sitting across from him.

Before either man could answer, the tannery bell rang, calling them to work. Some grumbled at the interruption, determined to hear the details from the scoundrels as the men cleared the house and set off.

Walking together the short distance to the tannery building, the men's eagerness was for anything but the work they faced. Uppermost in their thinking were the details about what the two had done on Saturday night in Glens Falls. Jail! That was something they wanted to hear about.

Moody, caught up in the attention to the story of their Glens Falls escapade and night in jail, failed to say anything about the unconscious girl he nearly tripped over in the night. He'd turned the problem over to Miss Wickham like everyone always did and hurried on. He didn't want to miss another day of work and have his pay cut.

Nineteen

Since Dr. Martin agreed to stay for Hazel's applesauce pancakes before returning to North Creek, Gracie decided to walk over to the hotel to tell Ambrose the terrible news. She wanted to catch him before he left on errands. Fortunately he was still in his office. Unfortunately she would have to wait, for his bald head was tilted back with a wide striped sheet around his neck, a face full of lather and his barber standing by stropping his razor.

Ambrose smiled at her. "Come in, come in. I'll be with you in a few minutes."

"I can wait outside until you're done."

"It's all right, Gracie. Did you come over to meet Jenny's husband?"

"That's partly right," she answered and decided not to say anymore until the barber was finished and they were alone.

She never ceased to wonder at the changes Ambrose had made to the old hotel: new furnishings, the gas lights last fall, and now a barber on the premises. She watched the elderly, white-haired man, incongruously called Junior, deftly stroke the large face with a knife-like razor, the long enamel handle in the curve of his right hand. Ambrose's gold rimmed shaving mug with its hand painted fishing scene and his name in letters of gold sat on a shelf nearby. The barber finished with much slapping of spicy aftershave, quickly dusting his client's neck with powder. Then with a dramatic flourish, pulling off the sheeting like a magician revealing his prize, he exited the office for his miniscule shop off the lobby. The smell of aftershave filled Ambrose's office.

He spun around in his chair and said, "Now, what can I do for you, Gracie?"

She exhaled and consciously took a deep breath. "There's never a good way to tell bad news, Ambrose." She looked down at her freckled hands folded against the front of her dark skirt and then up at him. "Jenny is dead."

"How?" he gasped and abruptly stood up, his smile replaced with concern. "You're tired. Come sit down. Tell me what happened."

She sat in the chair he led her to and said, "Moody Bedell was late coming back to the boarding house last night and nearly stumbled on her body lying outside. At least that's what he told me."

"Moody killed her?"

"No." She shook her head. "I don't know. He seemed upset over finding her and thought she was unconscious. I knew immediately she was dead. Didn't tell him that. He carried her back to my office and then I sent for the coroner after he left."

"Good lord! How did she die?"

"She was strangled, Ambrose. Choked to death."

"Who would want to kill that young child?" Ambrose shook his head. "She couldn't possibly have enemies."

"You said her husband was here in the hotel. I need to tell him what happened."

"Of course. I'll have him sent for."

While they waited with thoughts of the young woman they had so briefly known, they said little, each considering who might have committed such a crime. It took only minutes before the door opened. As they stood up, Gracie saw closely for the first time a well-dressed man with a shoulder length mane of silky brown hair. He frowned, paused in the doorway and said icily, "Well?"

Ambrose introduced Miss Wickham and told him she had something to tell him, but before she could say anything the husband said, "I suppose this is about my wife." He added angrily, "She didn't come back last night."

"I'm sorry, Mr. Crane." She did not find it easy to go on with the terrible news although she kept her voice calm. "Your wife was found dead early this morning."

The arrogant pose he'd assumed in the doorway crumbled as he stared at her, paled and staggered to the chair Ambrose had been sitting in. "No. No. It can't be." He looked at both of them, blinking several times as he went from face to face before he covered his own with his hands.

To his bowed head Gracie told how she'd been called out in the early hours by the man from the boarding house that found Jenny on the ground. "The young man who found her said he didn't know who she was and believed she had fainted."

He said nothing as Ambrose explained that Miss Wickham was the one everyone turned to in a crisis, of her medical training, and how the two women met on the train coming from Saratoga. Jenny's husband remained silent, only shaking his head as if to negate the terrible news. Finally he sighed deeply in an apparent effort to compose himself.

Gracie again spoke to his bowed head. "She told me on the train why she was coming to the Adirondacks."

When at last he looked up at her she heard the bitterness in his voice. "Ah, yes. The brother."

Ambrose said. "I was told her brother returned last night. He'll need to be notified as well."

"I've never met this brother she came to find." There was anger again in the tone of his words that seemed to blame Lewis LaPierre for Jenny's coming to the Adirondacks and what had happened to her.

That the brother was back was news to Gracie. "Neither have I," she said. She then added, looking at Crane, "You're free to come to my house where you can speak with the coroner for any questions you may have. But he'll be leaving shortly." She made to reach for her cape on one of the chairs to indicate she was leaving.

"Wait!" He stood suddenly and said, "My partner. I have to tell him."

"You can telegraph from here," Ambrose said.

"No! No. He arrived last night."

"Your partner is here?" Gracie was surprised to hear that the two men from Saratoga were both on the scene last night.

"I left word I was going to North Creek and didn't know he came to join us. Not until this morning. This is terrible. I'd better go speak to him."

"You can tell him right here," said Ambrose who looked at Gracie to see if she agreed.

Galvin Swagger was sent for and entered the office where the three waited. From his appearance she thought his name should be shamble rather than swagger. He was a rumpled, heavy man, his large head made larger by the swath of salt and pepper hair, like a sultan's turban, that added to his overall size. His genial smile and avuncular manner at introductions changed immediately when he heard what happened.

"Good God, Eddie, what did you do?" His wide nostrils flared like a bull at a red cape as he turned toward his partner.

"Hold on, Galvin. I'm not responsible."

"Then who is?" The two men looked at Miss Wickham as if she had the answer.

"That's what we intend to find out," she said crisply, and added, "I have no idea if Lewis LaPierre knows about his sister." She picked up the cape she had dropped on the chair and told them she had to leave and would send word for the brother.

Ambrose left the two men to walk her out to the lobby and ask, "Did you believe the husband's surprise was real? His grief?"

She looked into his light blue eyes. "I've never met the man before so it's hard to say. And now to learn his partner was here last night..." She didn't finish her thought.

"Makes you wonder, doesn't it?"

"Swagger was quick to suspect Crane, wasn't he?" she said. "Almost too quick."

"They're both con men," said Ambrose, shaking his head in disgust.

"I don't know how long the coroner will stay, and Jenny's brother must be told." Meeting Jenny's husband had been unsettling and now there was another man in her life Gracie had yet to meet and tell the dreadful news. "I should go, Ambrose."

"Of course." Ambrose returned to his office, while Gracie went out and stood on the porch, holding on the railing to think for a minute. That pause gave Annie O'Shea time to find her.

"Oh, Miss Wickham. It's a terrible thing, but I didn't do it!" Annie almost fell upon her as she rushed up.

Was she talking about Jenny? "What are you talking about?"

"The blue dress."

"What blue dress? What terrible thing?"

"I was sent upstairs to tell Dr. Crane Mr. Baldoon wanted to see him."

"And?"

"The blue dress. It was all ripped up and lying there in the hall outside her room. But I didn't do it." She was rubbing her hands over and over as if she was washing them.

"Why would anyone think you did, Annie?"

Annie colored and lowered her head. When she looked up, her gentian blue eyes filled with tears. "I went to her room yesterday. Before her husband came. I wanted to peek in her closet and I took out that blue dress. Just held it up to the mirror, that's all." Annie's distress and her thick brogue tumbled her words erratically between deep, inhaling breaths.

"That's all I did. I didn't tear it or anything. Or throw it in the hall like that. What will she say when she finds it?"

Gracie wondered how any of this fit in with Jenny being found on the ground last night. Obviously Annie had no idea what had happened to Jenny. Or did she?

"Did you see Jenny last night, Annie?"

Her wide eyes appeared innocent as she said, "In the dining room, yes. Saw when she left all mad and Sam followed her. That was the last time. Did she tear it herself? Knew I handled it? Oh dear, oh dear…" Annie's tears turned into sobs. Gracie put a hand on her frail shoulder to reassure her.

"Calm yourself, Annie, and thank you for telling me." She watched Annie go back inside the hotel, her shoulders shuddering. She might be innocent of destroying the dress but she had just placed Sam Somerville as the last one to see Jenny alive.

Cora Collins stood waiting on Miss Wickham's wide front porch. "Hazel said you'd gone to the hotel. Saw the coroner's buggy early this morning but Hazel's as tight lipped as a sealed jar. Why is he still here?"

Gracie thought of how she would answer and knew whatever she said would be passed around the boarding house. She studied the matron's face and said with a calm voice, "I understand Lewis LaPierre returned last night, Cora. I need to see him."

"He's gone to work. You gonna tell why the coroner's here? She's dead, ain't she?"

Gracie was shaken by Cora's correct assumption. "What do you know, Cora?"

"Know that Moody came back and found some woman on the ground unconscious. Had to knock to get in cause it was so late. Know Frenchy waited outside to meet his sister last night after he got back and sez she never showed and then I see the coroner's buggy. Don't need to know anything. Just guess."

Lewis LaPierre had waited outside for his sister? She'd only learned he had returned, and now to hear that he waited outside to see her? That could be damning. It was his word that they never met. Or had they? She disliked thinking this way. Or was Cora just being mischievous and knew more than she was telling. She needed to talk with the boy as soon as possible.

She didn't want to antagonize Cora. On the other hand she wasn't ready to give out any information so she said firmly,

"When her brother comes in at noon tell him I'd like to see him. Will you do that, please?"

"You ain't gonna tell me any more, are you?" and Cora crossed her fat arms and stomped off.

Twenty

Over the years men had studied the river and mastered the course needed to rush the loose logs to their destination. Eighty miles of the Upper Hudson River were fed by the tributaries of the Goodnow, Cedar, Indian and Boreas rivers, creating a tumultuous brawl of foamy white water in early spring. Below the hamlet of North Creek its rush of frothy rapids would intermittently disappear until the Schroon River's confluence with the Hudson at Warrensburg changed the flow, becoming more placid as it steadily moved on.

Once the river drive superintendent, John Dillon, gave the word, the lumber and paper companies sent their market logs endwise, one after another, pouring into the maelstrom of thousands and then hundreds of thousands of pieces of timber advancing with the current that would eventually reach Glens Falls. Before they reached the big boom that trapped them all, smaller booms waited with men on rafts of chained logs ready to shunt lumber to the saw mills that claimed them by their punched markings. Logs from Newtown Lumber and Nexus North, but also from the Rich Company, King Woods, and others totaling some ten different firms, were in the one drive. At times they mixed if a camp couldn't move logs ahead fast enough before another firm's logs, hard on their heels, joined them.

"I'll be meeting my family at The Glen when the drivers pull in for the night. All the locals come to see us." Paddy had spoken of this so many times that Tebo was beginning to feel he knew each one of them.

The young French Canadian who had attached himself to Paddy, Anton Theibault, smiled and nodded. He'd been quickly nicknamed Tebo. Dark haired, dark eyed, well built and strong, a follower rather than a leader which suited Paddy just fine.

"Whenever you see whitewater there's a rock downstream," he told him at the start of the drive. "You want to be looking ahead all the time." He also liked Tebo's interest in everything Paddy had to say and Paddy had a lot to say as if he were a lecturing professor.

The river was dotted as far as they could see with huge logs. The drive was strung out for miles, while all along the banks husky river men prowled, peavey or pike pole in hand.

"Keeping the logs moving and preventing jams from forming is the job of every river man. Deflecting the logs with ten foot pole pikes. Know the difference, Tebo. Cant hooks resemble peaveys but have a blunt end instead of a sharp spike."

Tebo nodded. He wore caulked boots called Croghans like the other men; stiff leather boots to prevent slipping, over his thick wool socks that still meant wet feet when he was out on the river. What did keep men warm were the union suits they wore all winter under heavy wool shirts and pants.

The Hudson River Gorge below Newcomb with rapids typical of many glacier-gouged rivers dropped in steps. Any stream with a vertical drop of two inches would bubble and slurp, and they had just experienced descents from Indian River to the Boreas of thirty feet per mile. That meant swift currents and white froth had to be negotiated. When a calm stretch came after two big vertical descents in the river, Paddy suggested it was time for a short break.

"We can ride the logs at this safe spot."

At river's edge Paddy picked out a fat log for each of them and with his sharp pointed peavey dragged them over so that the end of the log was out of the water and he could read the company's punch mark.

"Both these logs came from Nexus North," Paddy said. "See—it's got this x inside the large N."

"Looks kinda like a butterfly," Tebo said. He enjoyed imagining animals in several huge boulders along the river that looked like the backs of turtles. When he saw a mass of submerged boulders together he wondered aloud if it could be the back of a drowned dinosaur.

Paddy had laughed and decided Tebo was more fun than his own serious brother, Sam, would ever have been on the drive. Still, he was anxious to see Sam along with the rest of the family downstream. And he hoped his sister, Kate, would be well enough to join them.

"From turtles and dinosaurs to butterflies." Paddy threw his head back and laughed. "You're a fanciful fella." He straddled the log as he spoke and holding his pike shoved off and indicated Tebo was to do the same. It would be a short respite after the churning channels they'd come through. The day was sunny and cool with a damp breeze that felt like Father Winter's breath, but Paddy thought it was pleasant all the same. As they rode the peaceful stretch of a few miles among a sea of slowly moving spruce, they poked and prodded shore-bound stragglers. Paddy explained that some men thought it fun when riding to try to push each other off the log.

"Birling it's called. Might see it further down below Warrensburg where the river is slower and the worst dangers of the drive are over."

Sitting on their logs side by side with the current carrying them along, Paddy told the story of Gus Somebody birling last spring with another Frenchy.

"Mean bastard, that Frenchy was. Pushed old Gus toward some boulders and Gus lost his hold."

"You saw it?"

"Heard."

"And?"

"Couldn't swim. Wife and six little Gus Somebodys waiting back at Crown Point. Gus had no business fooling around like that. Frenchy bastard didn't even attempt to save him. After that he was poison and wherever he showed up everyone froze him out. No one wanted to be seen talking to him and story is one day he left camp without a word. Guess he got the message."

There'd be no birling in this stretch Paddy told him, which wouldn't last long anyway and his new friend was to watch for the signal to jump to shore before they approached any rapids.

"Watch the tops of trees on either shore," he shouted above the crunching sounds of logs ahead rubbing against each other and adding to the river's rumblings.

"You said to watch for rocks," Tebo shouted back.

"Yeah, but you can take a minute to look along shore. See if the treetops descend. If they're suddenly out of sight, you've got rapids coming up because it's a big drop. That's what they mean when they say reading the river."

Tebo grinned back and reached to take out his pipe.

"There'll be time for that," said Patty. "We'll be getting off soon. Just wanted you to see what riding was like. When you hear the men talk later about birling you'll know what they mean."

Tebo didn't put his feelings into words, but his eyes shone with affection for the big Irishman who'd befriended him.

"Rapids coming up at this next bend. That's when we'll get a jam. Better stay here and I'll catch you later."

Tebo had seen men standing on logs out in the river with their pipes, but he put his away and followed Paddy's signal to head for shore. When they reached it, they poked the logs back to join the rest.

Paddy looked up the river at the bobbing carpet of logs. He set off dancing atop the shaggy backs of the great herd, crossing the width of the river until Tebo saw him wave his pike in the air from the other side. From the western shore it looked as if the logs had piled below where Paddy stood and in the distance it looked as if the logs were caught up on a boulder.

He knew Paddy wanted a chance to be oarsman in one of the flat boats used to break up a jam. Had told him that last night after a dinner of ham and beans standing by a roaring fire in a cold drizzle. Looked like Paddy was going to get his wish. Volunteers had been asked for and after a time he could see Paddy with his red neck handkerchief getting into the jam boat. Would they use dynamite if the key log wouldn't move?

Twenty-One

Returning home from the hotel, Gracie considered the best way to break the news to Lewis LaPierre about his sister's death. She'd never met the boy and the little Jenny had said didn't indicate how close they'd been before she left home. Cora's news that the brother had gone outside to meet Jenny was unsettling, if true. The brutal way Jenny was killed would make it harder to tell him if he'd been waiting there and could have saved her. And any minute Ambrose would be bringing over Jenny's husband. Would Lewis suspect Jenny's husband? After seeing the faded bruises on Jenny's body, the coroner did. Would Jenny have written about physical abuse to her brother? Had anyone told him about the scene when Jenny wouldn't go up to their room with her husband?

Hazel was in the kitchen with Dr. Martin so Gracie answered the front door herself. She hadn't expected Moody Bedell to be with Jenny's brother, and it was he who spoke first.

"Miss Wickham?" Moody still looked the worse for wear. "You sent word you wanted to see Frenchy and I was wondering about that woman I found. Is she all right?"

Gracie looked at the man standing next to Moody. "You are Lewis?"

He was dark haired like his sister but summoned from work he was as dirty and sweaty as Moody, and appeared uneasy at being summoned. He was reluctant to speak and simply nodded to identify himself. An uncomfortable silence existed while Moody fidgeted with his cap.

"They told me when I got back last night she'd come lookin'." When he finally smiled, Lewis LaPierre's face was transformed into just short of handsome and boyish. He had very good teeth except for a few spaces in the bottom.

Gracie spoke to the brother rather than answer Moody's question. "Yes. And was found outside by Moody last night."

"Didn't say it was my sister." He looked darkly at Moody, but Moody hadn't made the connection or been given a name when he carried her body back to Miss Wickham's house.

Gracie interrupted what Moody was about to say and looked at Jenny's brother. "Moody didn't know. I regret someone did her great harm."

A shadow crossed her brother's face and he swallowed before speaking. "Will she be all right?" This dirty young man was the reason Jenny had come to the Adirondacks.

"I sent word to the hotel I'd meet her but she never came," he said.

There was no kind way to say it. She looked at the two young men and said, "She's dead."

Moody Bedell staggered as if he'd been hit from behind and let his hat drop to the floor. He fell against his roommate who paled from the impact of Moody's body or word of his sister's death, or both.

"How? Why?" Gracie heard the brother's pronounced French Canadian accent as he bolstered his friend and his voice trembled in shock or fear, she wasn't sure. "Steady," he said to Moody.

"We don't know why." She wanted to soften the terrible news by saying something about his sister. "She was so pleased when we saw your name at the tannery. Anxious to tell you about inheriting your uncle's farm." Gracie studied their stunned faces. There'd been no way to make it easier. "Her husband will be joining us soon. I understand you were unable to go to their wedding."

She could see the confusion in the brother's dark eyes. It was his long silence and bewildered staring that left her feeling uneasy. It must be too much for him to take in all at once. She tried to recall how many years younger Jenny had said he was.

What bothered her further was the inheritance. She'd picked up Jenny's reticule when she followed Moody back to the house. Examining it while she waited for the coroner revealed the deed to the farm that Jenny once had in it was missing. Where was it?

Another worry was Sam Somerville. Ambrose said Sam's wagon was still tied up at the hotel last night after saying he was headed home. They all saw how Sam was attracted to her when he stopped in at the hotel. And the waitress Annie said she'd seen him follow Jenny outside. But Sam's wagon wasn't there this morning and Jenny was dead. What reason could he possibly have for not going home as he intended?

By morning Margaret learned there'd been an accident but hadn't questioned Dr. Martin's presence beyond that. Hazel's scowl when her cousin probed ended further inquiries. It was Miss Wickham's business and hearing that guests were coming, Hazel sent Margaret on an errand to the general store to get her out of the house. No telling how she'd carry on about murder a few feet from the door while she slept. If Margaret got into her usual gossip with the genial shopkeeper she'd be gone awhile and not make a nuisance of herself. That could complicate things when the husband and brother met at the house for the first time.

Ambrose knocked and then stepped into the parlor to announce Jenny's husband was with him. His partner sent word he had no desire to meet Jenny's brother and would remain at the hotel.

After sober introductions all around, Gracie said, "Dr. Martin's in the kitchen. He'll be joining us."

Edward Crane had recovered his initial shock at Jenny's death enough to have resumed his theatrical manners. To Gracie the husband and brother were a contrast in styles. Certainly their clothes, the one so obviously a laborer who acted unsure with searching eyes one minute, and a nervous smirk the next, measuring the man so expensively dressed. His

109

instant ill-disguised dislike of his sister's husband made her wonder if it was just the clothes or if he knew some secrets Jenny had shared.

Oblivious to the boy's scrutiny, Edward Crane took the stage. "Well, young man, I've heard a lot about you." The boy's eyes narrowed but he didn't respond in kind, which Gracie believed unnerved the husband. Had Jenny written him about physical abuse? Was that why Jenny had been looking for her brother? As a way out of her marriage?

Margaret returned from her errand and peeked around Dr. Martin for a quick look at the assembled guests as Hazel jerked her away by the arm. The coroner heard their voices and entered the parlor. After introductions once more, he briefly explained he'd be taking Jenny's body to his North Creek office for further examination. "We need to wait to hear from the constable who is away at the moment."

No one questioned the coroner's dictum, accepting his brisk manner when he said he expected them to be available when needed. Perhaps it was Dr. Martin's tone, Gracie thought, but neither the husband nor brother had asked to see Jenny's body. Odd, that. Too uncomfortable, too shocked or feeling guilty that she'd met death by coming to find her brother?

"I'll see myself out," the coroner said after telling them he'd been up all night. He'd already told Gracie he expected her to investigate until the constable's return. Frowning at those gathered in the room, the small white-haired doctor made his exit.

Gracie released a big sigh, closing the door on the last of her guests, who seemed to have little to say once the coroner left. As tired as she was, she felt she should delay an early bedtime, afraid she'd wake after only an hour's sleep and lie there going over all who knew Jenny and might be involved in any way in her death.

When she finally retired she experienced a restless night with a dream that came shortly before dawn, that hour before waking when dreams are vivid and can be remembered. She was in the parlor of the tannery boarding house asking the different young men to write Jenny a letter about leaving logging camp. Each one came up to her and put their x on the paper she held in her hand, pushing it against her angrily. Didn't she know they couldn't write their own names? Someone had to write letters for them.

Jenny's husband came into the dream. Surely he could write? His partner? Jenny's brother? Sam? They were all there. Yet none of them could do anything but push an x onto the paper and shout at her to be left alone. To keep out of their business. She felt herself being pushed back and back and telling them to stop. Shouting it. Stop! You must stop. The words struggled from her in a muted moan, as they frequently do when emerging from a nightmare. Waking her.

It was unpleasant to consider what the dream meant, if anything. Men pushing her away, telling her to mind her own business? Women were often told that. But what struck her as she came fully awake was that it hadn't occurred to her to ask Lewis LaPierre for a sample of his writing. But what good would it do if Lewis had asked someone to write Jenny's letter for him? Did it matter whether Lewis had written the letter himself or asked someone to do it? He was here working in a tannery just as he said in the letter. Was she missing something? Did the sense she had that Lewis disliked Jenny's husband come from something Jenny might have written him? No, she wouldn't ask to see his handwriting, but she did have questions for him.

Rumors started Tuesday. It was inevitable that local men began looking at each other suspiciously when gossip said a young girl had been strangled. Where had they been between nine and ten on Monday night? Moody Bedell had stumbled on Jenny's body in the wee hours, but time of death had been established earlier by the coroner from when rigor mortis set in. Gracie let that information be known, answering questions by asking instead for any helpful information to solve Jenny's death.

Whispers began. Guarded looks. Sideway glances. Talk at the general store. Hushed conversations at the boarding house. Disagreements that became quarrels. Friendships suspected, and all trying to remember or prove where they'd been when Jenny was killed. Fear looked for a scapegoat.

"Had the peddler been back on the road?" someone asked her.

"No," she answered." Micah Rubin is at Blue Mt. Lake with his sister for the winter and won't take to the road again until early May." She found herself relieved that the peddler couldn't be blamed. Not everyone heard Jenny's husband and his partner were at the hotel the night before, and so far gossip hadn't targeted them. But if it became known Sam Somerville was the last one seen with Jenny, it could raise questions.

At the hotel she told Ambrose she needed to see what Sam had to say and planned to drive out to the farm. "Before Annie tells anyone else that Sam was the last one seen with Jenny."

Twenty-Two

As she headed out to the Somerville farm, Gracie drove the buggy slowly to avoid splattering road mud on her vehicle, her eyes on the horse's muscled rump in front of her; Jenny's murder and the dream she had last night on her mind.

The April day had warmed and rivulets of water seeped from hidden ground springs. Mist hung low between mountains to the east, with chalk white birches clear against the dark pines of rugged slopes. Evening rain had taken away more of the snow and white-washed the sky to a blue grey with wisps of smoky clouds, wind-driven and ever changing. A flock of slate-colored juncos soared into the air at the sound of rattling wheels, their conspicuous outer tail feathers like a V of white arrows shot into the sky.

The sound of an approaching vehicle caused her to look ahead where a wagon had pulled to the side. She came up to it at a slower pace, intending to pass. Instead, shouted greetings came from her neighbors, Maura and Orrin Rooney, who lived in the tannery tenancies. Maura, round and always cheery. Orrin, tall, thin and taciturn. The proverbial Jack Sprat couple.

Maura called out, "Miss Wickham! Heard 'bout that girl got killed. Know who done it?" Then a wide grin. She held her hand on Orrin's dark jacket to make him wait for Miss Wickham's answer.

Gracie fought her irritation. Did Maura expect information as if she had asked for something as simple as the correct time? Had they just come from the Somerville farm?

113

"Anything you know that can help, Maura?" It was the same answer she'd given over the last day and the same surprise she saw in Maura's face from answering one question with another. She touched the horse's flank lightly while Maura's mouth still held a surprised O and Orrin shook his head negatively. With a smile and a wave she moved on before Maura could recover and ask where she was headed. Word of the murder had traveled quickly and she wondered if Sam already knew about Jenny's death. Until she knew Sam's actions after leaving the hotel Monday night she didn't want to call attention to her destination and encourage Maura's curiosity. Or anyone else's.

Several scrawny brown chickens were pecking in the yard mud at the Somerville farm and she could hear hammering coming from the barn where the oldest brother, Johnny, would be working. From Sam's mother she learned she'd have to wait until he returned from hauling bark, so she went upstairs to visit. The recovering Kate sat in a rocker by the window with a book and shawl on her lap. Her bedroom was a small dormer room wallpapered with trellised pink roses on an ivory background.

"What are you reading, Kate?"

"Louisa May Alcott's *Little Women*. I like the one called Jo."

"You would. She's the tomboy."

"Thought you were going to bring that woman looking for her brother," Kate said, and added mischievously, "Sam had a lot to say about her looks."

"Did he? As a matter of fact I came to see Sam."

Kate's eyes looked merry when she said, "Sam's not as innocent as he looks."

Would Kate say that if she knew the errand Miss Wickham was on? She had to concentrate on what Kate said next.

"The girl's brother come back, Miss Wickham? Sam said you found his name at the tannery."

"We did." She rose and looked out the dormer window and was glad to see Sam rumbling into the drive below with his

114

buckboard. His sister apparently didn't know what had happened and Gracie, reluctant to get into it now, excused herself and hurried downstairs. Sam was surprised to see her and said so.

"I need to talk with you, Sam. Let's walk on over to the barn." He looked at her quizzically as he led the horse to the water trough and she followed.

"You were headed home from the hotel Monday night but Mr. Baldoon said your wagon was still there when he went outside."

"That's what you want to talk about?"

"I was told Jenny's husband was upset when he found you talking with Jenny at the hotel."

Sam's face colored. "Yes, he was. But all we did was talk. She wanted to know about logging camp. I couldn't tell her much. Didn't know her brother."

Gracie studied Sam's face. Was it possible he didn't know what happened to Jenny? "I understand that Jenny was unhappy with her husband and left the hotel in anger."

"She was. I thought she was going back to the boarding house but changed her mind, I guess. Last I saw she was looking to cross the road to the store."

That could be checked with the storekeeper, David Austin. "Did you stay to wait for her to come back?"

"Why would I do that?" Sam looked at her curiously.

"Because your wagon was still there."

"The front wheel wobbled when I started up. Couldn't trust it not to break down before I reached home. Went to see if the livery was open."

"Was it?"

"Why are you asking me all these questions, Miss Wickham?"

"You haven't heard that something happened to Jenny Crane that night?"

"What?" For the first time Sam Somerville showed concern. "What happened to her?"

"She was strangled, Sam."

"What?" He paled and mumbled, "Who would do such a thing?"

"That's what I'm trying to find out. You were the last one seen with her and you didn't go home right away." She quickly realized she hadn't been tactful.

"You think I harmed her?" his loud voice almost a shout. His face went from pale to flushed. "Why would I do that?"

"You said you went to the livery for help. Did Mott Sullivan fix the wheel?"

"Closed up. Took a chance. Went my way." His face had become a map of misery. "Poor woman. Pretty, too." Embarrassed, he looked down at his feet. "Don't tell Melissa I said that."

Melissa Eldridge was his childhood sweetheart and a friend to his sister, Kate. Gracie heard that when Melissa graduated from finishing school in Glens Falls the romance had cooled.

"Little chance of that, Sam. Melissa's still in Glens Falls, isn't she?"

"Yes, ma'am."

"I'm sorry I brought you this news. But I needed to find out if you knew anything that could help."

"Wish I could have helped her." He began unfastening the horse's straps as he scowled at Gracie, obviously annoyed she suspected him of doing harm. After a long minute he swallowed hard and in a husky voice said, "Hope you find the person who hurt her."

Back at the hotel Gracie tied her horse to the railing and went inside looking for Ambrose to tell what she'd learned from Sam. "I can check with Mott Sullivan at the livery, although I'm inclined to believe what he told me," she said.

"Want me to go with you?" Ambrose said.

"You're busy. I'll stop in at the store and see if David Austin saw her that night or if anyone followed her." She hesitated and then went on to tell him what Annie said about finding the torn dress in the hall without revealing Annie'd been in the room.

Ambrose said, "If it belongs to Jenny, I could ask him to identify it."

"Mind if I stay and hear what he says?"

The husband was sent for and after pausing in the doorway with a frown, looked startled when he saw the blue dress on the office desk.

"Yes, it's Jenny's dress." He spoke coldly. "Before you ask, I tore it and threw it out in the hall." He looked directly at them. "I was furious that she didn't return. Took it out on the dress, you could say."

"Did you go out looking for her?" Gracie thought that would be a logical thing a worried husband would do.

"No. I nursed my sorrows throughout the night." He looked at the dress. "When I woke and found she hadn't come in, well, you see the dress." He played with the floppy silk cravat at his neck as he spoke, revealing more nervousness than he was aware of. "Left it for her to find."

Yes, they saw the dress, but she was remembering the bruises on Jenny's body that he might not have realized she had seen. No wonder Jenny refused to go upstairs with her husband when she'd already angered him by being seen talking with a young, attractive male like Sam Somerville. Had anyone seen the husband leave the hotel and go out into the night? Even if no one saw him leave his room, he was the logical suspect. It looked as if his motive could be nothing more complicated than uncontrolled and deadly passion.

The husband's next words interrupted her thoughts and surprised them both. "I suppose I should talk to her brother about making funeral arrangements. I understand they call him Frenchy. Jenny always called him Lewis."

Of course the family had to make funeral arrangements once the coroner released Jenny's body. She doubted Jenny's brother could contribute to the expense but it was a decent gesture from the husband that she hadn't expected.

Ambrose gave him directions to the brother's boarding house and when the men would be finished work. They both watched him leave the office. "Well, Gracie, what do you think? An angry husband? A crime of passion?"

"It looks like it, doesn't it? That could be the motive. But how do we prove it? With a torn dress? And the old bruises? Unfortunately many husbands believe that kind of treatment is acceptable behavior."

Gracie bit her bottom lip as she thought about the husband planning to talk with the brother. It was time to share thoughts that couldn't be dismissed. Ambivalent thoughts she held about Lewis LaPierre.

"Ambrose! Suspend disbelief for a minute. What if the brother argued with Jenny about the farm? Suppose she wanted her share so she could leave her husband. Wanted to sell it and the brother didn't. What if that led to a fatal argument?"

"Her brother?" Ambrose shook his head. "Trouble with that, Gracie, is that Jenny didn't know her brother was back. Phonse Roblee came with the message Lewis would see her after Jenny stormed out of the hotel. As far as we know, she never got the message. Looks like she didn't meet up with him."

And the brother had said he waited for Jenny and she never came. "Who did she meet up with then? That is the question, isn't it?" Gracie asked.

She stood to go, unhappy with more questions than answers in the mystifying death.

Twenty-Three

Gracie walked into her front parlor in time to hear raised voices in the kitchen sounding like what Hazel called 'a spat.' She placed her heavy cape on the wooden clothes tree by the front door and walked to where the voices had grown louder.

"Well, I don't know as I remember that," Margaret said.

"I imagine that's so," Hazel answered.

"The man would probably appreciate my services." Margaret's voice overrode her cousin Hazel's as they stood facing each other by the sink.

"This is no time to be bedeviling the gentleman," Hazel shot back.

Gracie stood in the doorway unnoticed and asked, "What's this about?"

Her housekeeper turned and said, "Oh, it's you, Gracie. Margaret has a scheme for money making and I say this is not the time."

Bedeviling what gentleman? Services for what man? "Why don't you explain it, Margaret?" And with that Gracie sat down and pulled out a chair inviting Margaret to join her at the table.

Margaret plumped herself down, shifting her weight on the seat, and assumed a sorrowful face to accompany her words. "Got thinking about the Missus', poor child."

It had been left to Hazel to explain what had befallen Jenny Crane, choosing how much Margaret needed to know. Whatever loud reaction she had at the news had been kept from Miss Wickham's hearing. Now, after Hazel's admonitions to

119

keep her opinions about Jenny's death to herself, Margaret had come up with an idea. "You know, her raven hair and all," she said.

Gracie's puzzled face obviously called for some explaining.

"Mourning hair, she's thinking of." Hazel ignored Margaret's scowl.

"I did it when the boys went off, don't cha know." This was directed to Miss Wickham. Margaret turned away from Hazel to show she could ignore someone, too. "Family saved a lock for remembrance and if he didn't come back, it could be plaited. For a keepsake. Watch fob, ladies' pin, wreaths, bracelet, all kinds of things."

"She thinks the mister would like some of his wife's hair."

"Mr. Crane?" So that's what the cousins were arguing about. A remembrance from Jenny's hair. "Margaret, you're suggesting you want to make a piece of mourning jewelry to present to Jenny's husband? Do you have some of her hair? I didn't know you knew her."

"She doesn't. Didn't," said Hazel. "Just saw her here that one time. Been talking about making herself some money and thinking about how." Hazel's pursed lips told what she thought of the plan.

"Excuse me for trying to earn my keep," Margaret sniffed. Margaret hadn't found employment since the death of her employers last autumn.

"No one's asked you to pay board." Hazel looked at Gracie for affirmation. "Have we?"

Gracie nodded and smiled, which seemed to encourage Margaret to go on.

"If her husband would like a piece of mourning jewelry, Miss Wickham, we could tell Dr. Martin and he'd let us have some hair, wouldn't he?" Margaret raised her grey streaked eyebrows expectantly. "Whatever the mister wanted. Enough for a stick pin or ring or maybe cufflinks."

"And I say," Hazel interrupted, "doesn't even know the man. And it's not to everyone's taste."

But for some, a person's hair represented love and loss, and mourning mementos had grown in popularity through the war years. Articles in the popular *Godey's Lady's Book* waxed poetic: "Hair is at once the most delicate and lasting...so light, so gentle, so escaping from the idea of death that with a lock of hair belonging to a child or friend we may almost look up to heaven and compare notes with angelic nature...."

Margaret continued. "Haven't done it since the war but if Mr. Baldoon agreed, I could put some samples on display at the hotel. For people passing through, you know."

Before the war, *Godey's* magazine advertised, "...to accommodate any lady wishing hair made up into jewelry upon receipt of the hair and the price for making it."

It told that a full size bracelet called for hair 20 to 24 inches in length. Or brooches, cufflinks and bracelets could be made from the magazine's instructions and patterns.

Gracie looked at Margaret's aged-spotted hands with their arthritic knuckles. She'd heard Margaret complain, "I'll have it to the year one." Hair weaving required special wooden molds from a local wood turner, bobbins and weights to maintain correct levels and keep the hair straight. How realistic was it to think of returning to a craft she might once have been successful at. Maybe nothing would come of it but Margaret sat waiting for some kind of answer.

Gracie's face softened and she said, "I'll mention it, Margaret."

"See!" Margaret looked triumphantly at her cousin Hazel.

"Doesn't mean he'll say yes." Hazel crossed her arms for emphasis and turned her back, once again bending at the spotless sink that she began to scrub vigorously.

Gracie shook her head, stood and poured herself some chamomile tea and, setting aside thoughts of mourning hair, took it into her office at the back of the house. She was aware of a sense of urgency for what could be discovered before the constable, Jeremiah Russell, returned.

Obadiah jumped into her lap as soon as she settled into her father's big chair. The marmalade cat's loud purring and the soothing tea comforted her as she pondered suspects and motives, bits and pieces she gathered thus far. Sam Somerville's story of a wobbly carriage wheel and the need to borrow tools from the livery had checked out. Mott Sullivan had closed his livery and retired early and saw Sam walking away after Mott was struggling into his trousers to answer the door. And David Austin said Jenny had come into the store that night shortly before he was ready to close for the day.

"Pretty little thing, she was. Restless, moving about fingering fabric, studying cards of buttons. Not into conversation. Didn't stay long." The affable store owner loved conversation, talk and gossip. Gracie sometimes suspected he had bought the store for the social intercourse it brought him.

When the constable returned, he would in all likelihood arrest Jenny's husband without proof. People had begun to speculate. What kind of a doctor was Edward Crane? He gave no account for the evening his wife was killed other than saying he'd spent the night in his room drinking. No one had reported seeing him out and about and he was sticking with his story. On the other hand, if no one saw him outside, he could have strangled Jenny and simply not been seen. But it had been a bright night that evening. Or had clouds moved in at the moment Jenny faced her killer? Odd though that Mr. Crane didn't know his partner had arrived until the next morning.

She continued to sip her tea and think. What about Galvin Swagger? What time had he arrived at the hotel? Was it a coincidence he came to Wevertown the very night Jenny was murdered? The husband said he was going to talk with Lewis LaPierre about funeral arrangements, although Dr. Martin wasn't planning to release Jenny's body until the constable returned. Thinking of how long Jeremiah Russell had been away caused her to look at the large wall calendar across from where she was sitting and see the date with a big X for when the river drive was expected to reach The Glen.

The Somervilles would be gathering to meet Paddy there. Maybe he'd have something to tell about working with Lewis

LaPierre at Newtown camp. What was he really like? She had mixed feelings about Jenny's brother.

After the husband and Moody Bedell left, she'd asked Lewis why he left logging camp for tannery work. "Did you want to leave because of the log drive, Lewis? I understand it can be very dangerous."

"I'm not afraid of danger," his tone was cocky as if he'd been challenged. "Sure. It can be dangerous. Imagine trying to find your marked logs on a swollen river." His dark eyes seemed to dance as he spoke of the danger.

"I thought you said you'd never been on the drive, Lewis."

He stammered for a beat and said, "Right. I meant to say you can't imagine. That's what I meant to say. From what men at camp said I can guess how dangerous it would be. Anyway, I found work here."

He stood to go as if that ended the discussion. With an apologetic grin he said he had to leave. But he was lying about something. She wasn't sure what.

But she was uneasy about Edward Crane and Galvin Swagger as well. Was it her imagination or was there an unacknowledged antagonism between the partners? She sensed it between the husband and brother. Over what Jenny might have told her brother? Or over the deed? She was sure Jenny had brought the deed with her. Would it be in her room at the hotel? Had her husband ever seen it?

Her musings were interrupted with Hazel announcing Mary McCarthy at the house seeking advice. After Mary and the baby left with oil drops for the baby's ear, Gracie considered what Mary had told her. A chance remark that the boarding house matron had just left for shopping in Warrensburg.

She sat at her desk after seeing Mary out, considered the timing and realized she might never have such an opportunity. The tannery men would be at work and all she'd need do would be to explain to the cook she was returning the hat Moody Bedell dropped when he was at her house.

With Cora Collins out of the house, a search of Lewis LaPierre's room might reveal he had the deed. If he did, that would indicate he had met his sister no matter what Ambrose said about Jenny not getting the message the brother was back. Let Lewis explain that.

Twenty-Four

As light rain changed to soft, wet snowflakes, leaving a thin coat of white on the ground, Gracie set off for the boarding house across the road. She pulled her black cloak closer to shut out the dampness. The grey afternoon's visibility extended only a few yards as she peered through the flurry of wetness that made the low stone walls gleam. By the time she reached the back kitchen door, the flakes had returned to drizzling rain, and she thought once again how capricious was the month of April.

The landlady of the boarding house had left after the men's noon meal and would be back in time for evening supper that the cook was busy preparing. Chopping and cutting and muttering at the vegetables, or was it the young dishwasher the cook was speaking to? The cook was a small woman, bent over with osteoporosis.

A bone strengthening broth could help the woman. It was one Gracie had Hazel make for some of the patients. Cabbage, dandelion greens, nettle greens and pigweed could be gathered in good weather and brought to a simmer in a pot of water with fish bones. She considered mentioning this to the cook but realized she didn't have the time now. She'd like to write out the recipe though, for this woman could fracture a leg and not realize she was losing bone mass. So many women just accepted it with aging.

But it wouldn't do to have Cora walk in and ask what she was doing here and not get a chance to search the brother's

125

room. Gracie held up the hat. "Excuse me. I'm returning Moody Bedell's hat."

In a louder voice she added, "He left it at my house."

The cook grunted her reply, pointing to the stairs to indicate she couldn't bother over what Miss Wickham was about. Nothing was said about a search but with Cora out of the building that was exactly what Gracie intended to do.

She walked through the dining room with its long trestle table and benches on either side and came around to the entry hall, all quiet without the men who lived there. She stopped to glance into the parlor where she and Jenny had visited to talk to those playing cards the night they'd asked about Jenny's brother. With the men at work she wasn't expecting anyone to be there but wanted to reassure herself. She placed a hand on the railing, took a deep breath and raising her long, dark skirt, started up the stairs to the men's bedrooms.

She knew where Moody's room was because last year she'd brought a poultice for his infected toe when he wasn't able to walk across the road. Phonse Roblee was his roommate then and said he would have gone for the poultice for his friend Moody. No, she told him, she had come to see how the toe looked for herself. She'd made a wad of plant material after boiling and pounding it making a paste with water and flour, shaping it so it would lie flat against his toe. She had encased it in clean cloth to make a compress and wanted to show her patient how to hold it in place like a bandage. She liked Moody and saw how fatigued he was the night he discovered Jenny on the ground. He and Phonse appeared to be good friends.

Now Lewis LaPierre shared the room with Phonse and Moody. Glancing around the bedroom she felt uneasy, trying to decide which cupboard would hold the belongings of Jenny's brother. If he had the deed, it was likely hidden there. The room itself was clean with an almost prison-like sterility to it. No paintings on the wall to interrupt the stark, vertical lines of the pine boarded room. No brightly colored quilts. Instead, dark woolen blankets covered the single cots that stood out from the wall for easier bed making for the chambermaid.

She looked at each cupboard deciding that the one with the fewest possessions would belong to the newest arrival. Her movements were silent and careful; she was reluctant to disturb anything by her search. Underclothes and heavy socks were jumbled haphazardly in the cupboard she decided was Lewis LaPierre's. Lifting gently, she felt between layers of a few wool shirts and under clothes looking for a piece of paper that could be the deed Jenny spoke of, but found nothing. There was so little to look through that she was done in a few minutes. She stood in the center of the room and sighed. Perhaps she was wrong to suspect the brother of any wrongdoing.

But she remembered their conversation before he'd left her house on hearing his sister was dead. She'd told him Jenny showed her his letter on the train. "You said something about lumber camp not what you expected. Not like the farm, you meant?"

He'd avoided her eyes. "Yeah. Guess that's what I meant."

"You were going to let her know when you found tannery work, I believe."

"Yeah."

There was the grin again as he finally looked at her, demanding to be believed. His charm meant to convince. But she was convinced he was lying about something.

She sighed once more as she turned to close the cupboard door. Her foot struck something sticking out from under one of the beds. She started to push it back with her black boot but when it didn't move easily she bent down to see what it was. A handle of some sort? Twelve inches, maybe. Attached to what?

She didn't know whose bed it was. They all looked the same. She reached down and pulled the heavy wooden handle toward her. An axe? Attached was an iron head with a raised metal design, a diagonal in the center that looked to be a heavy marking hammer used to identify logs. The kind of tool a lumberman standing next to a pile ready for the skidway would hold, swing back, and with a heavy blow punch his company's log. But what lumber operation had for its identifying mark a diagonal slash? And which of the roommates did it belong to?

127

Footsteps were coming up the stairs and she held her breath. Her pulse was racing and she stood, reviewing what she would say if someone opened the closed bedroom door and saw her standing there. Quickly she pushed the marking hammer back, far under the bed this time and stood again, breathing slowly to calm herself. The steps were light and passed the door echoing down the wide hall toward the other dormitory like rooms. Probably a chambermaid bringing something to one of the rooms. Still, she'd rather not be seen and be forced to give explanations.

She waited until she heard the light steps descending the stairs and stepped out into the hall. She left the house without stopping to bid the cook goodbye. She had done what she told the cook she came for, to return Moody's hat, which she'd left in the parlor. No sense calling attention to the fact she'd been in the bedroom. She didn't enjoy this part of playing sleuth, choosing a time when Cora Collins wouldn't be there to accuse her of snooping. Which, of course, was just what she'd been doing. But Cora would have asked too many questions She hadn't found the deed but found something else that didn't make sense. Was someone keeping it as a souvenir? Was the punch mark to be used as a weapon of some sort? Had it been stolen from one of the logging camps? But no lumber company she knew of had a mark like that. And why keep it hidden under the bed?

Outside the ground was now white, covered in a half inch of wet snow that showed her tracks as she walked deliberately, her head bowed but her mind racing with more questions than answers. April's weather was changeable, like the ups and downs in her search for Jenny's killer. What would Ambrose say when she told him where she'd gone and why and what she had found instead of a deed? Would he have noticed such marked logs at the skidways he'd visited with John Dillon? Or would Ambrose come up with some simple explanation and simply shake his head at her wild assumptions?

Twenty-Five

A white-throated sparrow with its striped crown piped open his clear call: "Old Sam Peabody, Peabody, Peabody," a series of whistles that began his day from nearby riverside thickets. Already some of the men had quit the drive, discouraged by the long cold, wet days or near mishaps they experienced or had seen; men who decided to walk on out for home. Frosty days started at three in the morning with breakfast an hour later while they stood shivering by a fire waiting for early first light. Paddy was counting the days until they reached The Glen and he could see his family.

Tebo looked around the morning campfire at the other drivers standing in their patched woolen sweat shirts and yellow suspenders, red neck scarves, baggy cuffed pants torn so the cuffs wouldn't snag on limbs, those stiff leather boots made in Croghan, New York, over their wool socks, felt hats covering sweaty hair. Sometimes logs would become ensnared in backwater and then Tebo would meet men from other camps. He was beginning to recognize by name some of the drivers who had been choppers but were now all united in the one big river drive.

One hairy man someone called the Jokester actually did tell him a joke. Tebo wasn't sure he understood it or would be able to recall it to tell Paddy.

"I say, Mike, what sort of potatoes are you planting?" the Jokester smiled, revealing most of his teeth were missing.

129

"And Mike answers, 'Raw ones, to be sure. Ye wouldn't be thinking I'd plant boiled ones.'" The Jokester slapped his knee and laughed a high he-he. "Ain't that a dinger?"

But Tebo could usually remember a name because of some harrowing near-accident like what happened to Rube Lyman yesterday, who'd set out to clear some logs piled up deep. Someone yelled from the bank when thundering logs got loose and started to roll down on him.

"Watch out!"

Startled, Rube looked up and acted quickly. His first jump landed his left foot on a big spruce, but before he could bring up his other foot, another log bobbed out of the water and he was stuck between them, trapped!

"Hold on."

Paddy saw the fix the man was in and before the logs came thundering down on the frightened victim, ran out on the logs and jumped, landing hard on the log behind Rube. His force drove one end of the log deep into the water. The other end snapped up like a spark just missing Rube's head, but the action freed him. Seconds later the rollway that had threatened to smash him came rushing down to where he'd been trapped. Rube sailed off on the big spruce with a grinning Paddy standing upright on the other end. The men watching hooted and cheered. No need for Paddy to yell 'look at me' that day.

It was the kind of story that would be told over and over again long after the drive was finished and in future years when yarns were passed around campfires and smoky tavern rooms. But no one could save the man who died just before the drive came to Racehorse rapids.

"If he'd used his head..." Paddy swore.

The current had hit just enough to throw the man off balance and he fell into fast water, losing his stout lever with its sharp spike. He tried to grab a passing log but he had caught it by the middle.

"If he'd grabbed hold of the log at the end, he could have hoisted himself up and we'd of pulled him out," Paddy grumbled. "Kept trying to wrestle that log and it kept rolling out of his hands. Panicked. Wasn't using his head."

Paddy and some of the others had raced across the logs, ready to pull out the doomed logger. "But by the time we reached him, he'd let go. Shock of the cold water and all." Paddy took the red handkerchief from his neck and wiped his face. "Just went under and swept away." Not for the first time the men took up a collection for a widow.

Tebo thought he should remember the man's name out of respect, but for the life of him it escaped him. What he did remember was not to cross the logs without a good grasp on his pike pole.

By noon the drivers stopped to feed hungry stomachs at a quiet, sandy spot called Washburn Eddy. It took 4,000 calories a day to sustain a man, and the cook who traveled with them on shore had pork drippings on hardtack ready for a quick meal. Time out for coffee and beans and then back to work.

The sun came out from behind the clouds and the drive went on. Before long another jam pile-up happened. Logs were shoved, up-ended, and forced others aloft while the face of the jam rose higher, causing the tail of snaking logs upstream to grow swiftly dangerous. The call went out for volunteers. Tebo raised his eyebrows expectantly at Paddy. "Not this time." And with a negative shake of his head Paddy set off while Tebo watched.

It looked like Paddy was going to get his chance finally to be oarsman. The four-foot-wide jam boat was brought up and maneuvered into place. Two men sat front and aft, ready with their canter hooks and pikes.

Tebo saw the bowman hook onto a stuck log while Paddy jumped out and secured the boat. It took time to locate the key log.

"This one?" Balancing deftly, sweating.
"No. That one."
"Here?"
"Try it."
"Yes!"

131

Once found, they swung and chopped at it slowly, then listened. To avoid getting tangled in the lot, the three jumped back into the boat when it sounded as if the jam was breaking up.

But, no. "Damn it!"

The logs had stopped moving again. The air rang with their curses.

"Get the dynamite!"

Tebo watched, recalling what Paddy had told him about a river drive last year when the dynamite had frozen and they built a fire to thaw it out.

"Wasn't that dangerous?" he'd asked.

"Damn right, it was."

"What happened?"

"They built a bank of earth around the fire a few feet back, and stood the sticks of powder up against the inside of the bank. This young kid didn't use his head when one of the sticks slipped and fell toward the fire, and he reached over to pull it out."

Tebo gasped.

"Luckily, Old Gus strode up to see if the powder was ready and when the kid reached out, Gus grabbed him and flattened him to the ground like a pillow. Boom! Wham! That stick exploded all over the place!"

"Was anybody hurt?"

"Nobody! Kid was pretty shook, though."

"Was he let go?"

"Naw. Gus just wagged his head and told him to be more careful, s'all's."

Now Tebo watched from the boulder he was standing on and saw what Paddy was doing with the dynamite. Paddy'd get extra pay that day. The jam boat had been pulled back and Paddy had a long pole, maybe fifteen feet, with half a dozen sticks of dynamite lashed to its end. He skipped over the carpet of logs until he reached the hole he'd chosen and lit the waterproof fuse, then dashed to get out of the way as if he'd been shot out of a cannon.

Seconds went by. Then a cacophony of sounds: *Boom!* *Bang!* More rumbles and explosions as the whole front of the jam came crashing loose with a tumultuous roar and an outbreak of rioting men, as noisy logs exploded skyward and down river.

More cheers and hurrahs for Paddy who had earned his swagger.

His moment didn't last long. It was back to work, the job of every river driver poking and moving logs. It was still weeks away from the big boom at Glens Falls, but Paddy knew they were getting close to The Glen.

Twenty-Six

Despite the weather, drivers with wagons and carts rattled along the Wevertown road delivering hides and bark to men working in the tannery. Cora Collins continued her shopping in Warrensburg and Gracie hurried away from what she'd found at the boarding house. She strode briskly to the hotel, excited to share her discovery with Ambrose, realizing he had, in a short time, become her trusted confidante. Another discovery, she thought.

Inside the hotel she passed Annie O'Shea standing in the dining room and saw her turn abruptly away at Gracie's greeting. What was the matter now? The girl was usually so friendly. Had she not understood enough when Annie told her about the blue dress? Was the girl not feeling well? Drat! She'd look into it later. She knocked at Ambrose's office door and heard his deep voice call to enter.

"Gracie! You look flushed. Something wrong?"

She sank into a seat at the side of his desk. "Just a guilty conscience."

"You?" he let out a hearty laugh.

"Where to begin?"

"I'd say at the beginning." He smiled and leaned forward, inviting her to go on, resting his elbow on the desk with the palm of his hand against his cheek as if he had all the time in the world.

She began by telling him why she decided to go to the boarding house while Cora was away and what she had stumbled upon.

"Literally stumbled, that is."

"Are you sure it's a marking hammer of some kind?" Ambrose leaned back in his big swivel chair and fingered the gold chain of his watch.

"I can't think what else it could be."

"But you were searching for a deed and didn't find it?"

"No."

"Do you think Jenny kept it in her room?"

"She must have if it wasn't in her reticule."

"Easy enough to find out."

"You mean, search her room?" Was Ambrose serious? But the husband..."

"He went with Swagger to look at coffins in North Creek. Hired transportation from the livery."

"Look while they're gone?"

"It's murder, Gracie. If you think finding the deed will tell us something, well...I don't ordinarily go round searching in guests' rooms but this is not an ordinary situation."

They climbed the wide hotel stairway to the floor where Jenny had her room. Ambrose used his master key to enter. Jenny's lilac toilet water still lingered in the room, a faint scent Miss Wickham remembered from the time Jenny sat down on the train seat next to her.

The wardrobe stood against the wall where the blue dress Annie coveted had once hung. Gracie carefully lifted folded clothes in the dresser, searching for the legal paper. Ambrose, standing inside the doorway, raised his eyebrows, asking the question. She nodded negatively. He stepped further into the room and together they turned to the small writing desk for the search. After a few unproductive minutes, she gave up looking for the deed.

Ambrose held up an opened envelope he'd taken from the pigeon hole at the back of the desk, and tapped it against his lips, thinking.

"Maybe this can reveal something. It's a letter to Jenny."

"Perhaps it's the letter from her brother she read to me on the train."

He offered it to her but she saw immediately it was not the letter Jenny had produced on the train.

"You read it, Ambrose."

Aloud, Ambrose read, *"My dear Jenny, I spoke to your Edward before he set out to find you and he promised me to mend his ways. I will see that he does. You have my word on this.*

You are an integral member of our enterprise and the loss of your company grieves me deeply. It's time to come home. Sincerely, Galvin Swagger.

"It's from the partner," Ambrose returned it to the desk.

"I think it was sent with the husband to give to Jenny. I wonder if she ever saw it."

"Maybe not, but someone opened it and its further proof Edward Crane was an abusive husband."

Gracie shook her head. "And probably the cause for Jenny's excuse to go looking for her brother."

"You think the partner came to protect her from him?"

"Possibly. He sounds concerned."

"So, Gracie, it would appear the partner knew Crane was abusive. And you saw her bruises."

"Let's go, Ambrose." She looked around and added, "I've done enough snooping in other people's rooms to last a lifetime."

As they walked downstairs she said, "The fact we found no deed makes me wonder if there ever was one or was it a ruse to get away."

"Didn't she show it to you on the train?"

"From what she said on the train, I believe it existed and that she had it with her. She showed me her brother's letter and held on to a paper I thought was the deed. Maybe she wanted to sell her share in order to get away permanently. But it wasn't with her when we found her body."

"We'll never know." Ambrose opened the office door and swept his arm as invitation to enter.

"I won't come in. I should go to North Creek. Let Dr. Martin hear what I've learned so far. He's the one who asked me to look into this." She paused and smiled. "There's another reason, Ambrose. Margaret wants a lock of Jenny's hair."

"You're serious? Whatever for?"

She explained what Margaret wanted to do with mourning jewelry as a keepsake for Jenny's husband.

"You know, Ambrose, he seemed so upset at first. This might gauge the husband's true feelings."

"You think Dr. Martin will give it to you? Go ahead then, Gracie. But I'm not promising Margaret any business at the hotel."

The unpredictable April weather changed once again when the sun came out during the eight mile drive to North Creek. Ahead rose Gore Mountain with its snow-covered slopes still resisting signs of spring. She passed the Baptist church outside the village and turned the horse on to Main Street. On her right stood the large Straight House where the railroad workers stayed, and others who came into town for supplies. She'd heard talk the Methodists planned a church across the road.

People were out and about walking briskly in the cool air, intent on their errands. Farther down on the right, she saw the little tailor shop amid what some called the commercial block, the small and moderate sized buildings with retail stores at street level and living space above. Swain's funeral parlor on the right sold coffins upstairs. For all she knew the two partners were inside now.

A woman carried a package out of the butcher's shop. Above it was the second story's pool hall that did not allow ladies. There was the barbershop and the store for women's hats, and next to that the grain store and livery.

The American Hotel anchored the end of Main Street on the left. She heard a train whistle warning that a northbound train would soon be puffing into the station and realized street traffic would increase. She hurriedly pulled up to the horse block in front of the coroner's office and stepped down.

It was some time before Dr. Martin finished with a patient and before she could relate her lack of success in identifying Jenny's killer, as well as the news that Galvin Swagger had also come seeking Jenny. After hearing all she had to say, it was the coroner's opinion that the husband was guilty of killing Jenny whether in a passionate rage or by accident. The small white haired doctor studied her with his bright blue eyes. "It's usually the spouse, Gracie."

Dr. Martin wanted Jenny's husband held. "Until Jeremiah Russell is back and can charge Edward Crane," he waved his hand as if dismissing that it could be difficult, "Ambrose should be able to keep him there."

To her annoyance he also dismissed any importance to the partner's arrival on the scene or her discovery of a logger's mark in the boarding house.

But she was successful in one area by the time she left. Resting in tissue paper within her reticule was a long lock of Jenny's raven hair for Margaret. As she rode along in gathering twilight, her mind was on what Dr. Martin had said about Edward Crane. "It's usually the spouse, Gracie." If he was guilty, would he want such a remembrance of his wife in mourning jewelry?

Twenty -Seven

Gracie hurried up the hotel steps to tell Ambrose that Jenny's husband should be confined at the hotel until the constable returned. Inside, she saw Annie carrying a tray of clean glasses into the dining room where she set them down on a serving station table. Annie's shoulders slumped forward as if the weight of the empty glasses had been more than she could manage. It was not the posture of the cheerful Irish immigrant Gracie knew.

She followed her into the large room and called her name. Annie turned around, her blue eyes darting about the room as if to see who might be watching her. But the noon crowd had mostly finished and the few stragglers were leaving. Gracie noticed dark shadows under Annie's eyes, almost as black as the bombazine uniform she wore. The scattered freckles on her small nose stood out on her face, now almost as pale as her bibbed white apron.

Gracie drew closer to the frightened girl and softly said, "What's wrong, Annie? Not feeling well?"

"No. No. I'm fine."

"You don't look fine. Working long hours?"

Her voice broke. "It's not the hours. Just..." Her voice trailed off.

Gracie stood quietly, searching Annie's face, and waited.

Annie's eyes looked troubled. "Wish I'd never..."

"Never...?" she stopped. Gracie's serious brown eyes held Annie's blue ones. "You have a secret?"

Annie gasped. Agitated, she glanced around the room again as if checking to see who might overhear. "How do you know?"

Gracie said. "You told me about the blue dress. So that's not your secret. That's not what's bothering you, is it?"

"No. It's just...I know something I shouldn't," Annie whispered. "But not here." She drew closer and said, "Can I come over to your house? After work?"

"Of course. I'll wait for you to come when you're ready, Annie." She reached out to touch her hands and found them cold.

Chilled by the touch, she walked outside, pulling her dark cape closer. She stood on the hotel porch for a moment watching traffic rattle by in both directions, thinking of Annie's problem. Bark-loaded wagons headed east toward the tannery, while a buckboard left from Mott Sullivan's livery toward North Creek. But there was no sign of the constable, Jeremiah Russell, returning from the west. How much time did she have to solve Jenny's murder before his return?

What could be the secret Annie was afraid to talk about in the hotel? She was obviously fearful. Was it as simple as a problem with her work? She said it wasn't the work hours. Wished she'd never...? What? Did it have something to do with Jenny's murder? With her thoughts on the troubled young servant, she stepped off the wide porch and turned toward home.

Questions still bothered her despite Dr. Martin's view. What about the punch mark found in the bedroom Lewis shared with Phonse and Moody? Had Jenny's brother taken it when he left Newtown loggers? But their marker was simply a big letter N. For all that it could belong to one of the other roommates. But Dr. Martin hadn't thought it significant. He was convinced that only Jenny's husband was guilty and that's what mattered.

What about Phonse Roblee? Ambrose told her Phonse had delivered Lewis' message to have Jenny meet him. Phonse had been in the boarding house parlor when Jenny had inquired about her brother and seen how beautiful she was. Had he waited for her and a struggle ensued when she refused his advances? Was it something as simple as that to explain why her brother waited for her in vain?

Drat! In her concern for Annie, she'd walked out of the hotel without telling Ambrose the coroner wanted Jenny's husband held. Well, if Edward Crane was buying a coffin for his wife he wasn't going anywhere soon.

Hazel and Margaret were in the kitchen and looked up expectantly when she came in.

"You look like you could use a cup of tea," Hazel said and went to the stove while Margaret asked where she'd been.

"North Creek." She managed a weary smile and took out the small tissue wrapping of Jenny's locks and set it in front of Margaret. "Dr. Martin said you can offer it to her husband."

The cousins sat down at the table and looked at what Gracie had brought. Margaret unwrapped the tissue and was subdued as they all considered the inky strands.

"What do you propose to do with it, Margaret?"

She looked up at Miss Wickham with a false bravado. "Why, I'll talk to the mister, of course. Go to the hotel and ask him what he'd like made up for a keepsake."

"Maybe I could pave the way for you." She didn't want Margaret's feelings hurt by the theatrical Edward Crane ridiculing her. And she was interested in seeing for herself his reaction to the offer.

"Would you do that?" Margaret's relief showed in her enthusiasm.

"Yes, but right now I'm going to take my tea in the back office. I'm expecting the waitress from the hotel, Annie O'Shea, to stop by." To Hazel she said, "Bring her in when she comes, will you?"

Alone in her office she sank into the big chair behind the desk, glad to be able to think quietly. She'd like the chance to talk with Lewis LaPierre about his sister and was curious to learn more about him. In the short time she'd spent with him, she gathered he could be likable. He could be charming with his smile and dimples. Perhaps his good looks had spoiled his character and caused him to look for easy opportunities like gambling. Had Jenny and her brother been close?

Jenny said her brother was a few years younger. Did she look out for him when they were growing up? She seemed surprised to hear he'd won at cards. Would have been more surprised to know he spent a night in the Glens Falls jail which had come out later. Yet even with the same parents, children can be very different. She'd seen that with the families who came to her. The McCarthys with their lovely children; some restive, or ebullient, some calm and thoughtful.

Gracie rested her head back against the big chair and thought about what it would be like to have a brother. Was affection automatic or did most siblings feel competitive?

She recalled her friend Susan told her she was the second of seven children in her large Quaker family and close to her three sisters. What would it feel like to be a big sister, Gracie wondered? Would a younger brother be very different in looks and disposition from her? Have her carrot colored hair?

What was it like for Kate Somerville to have four older brothers? Then there was Kate's brother, Sam. Had it been too easy to dismiss Sam as a suspect because she'd known the family for years? Kate may have revealed more than she realized by saying Sam wasn't as innocent as he looked. Why hadn't she pursued that? What Sam told about trouble with his wagon delaying him meant it was possible he had time to confront Jenny, harm her and then drive off. Either Sam or Phonse could have accosted her, but that could be said for any of the young men who lived in the boarding house and seen the young woman.

The knock on the door interrupted her ruminating and reminded her that Annie was expected, but before Hazel could announce Annie's name, Lydia Finley announced herself and marched into the room.

"Lydia! What a surprise. How are you?"

As always, the bookkeeper's wife was dressed in the latest fashion. She wore a shimmering taffeta matching jacket and skirt in grey with black geometric braiding on cuffs and hems. Her lacy black neck jabot quivered with her indignation as she answered. "Upset, Miss Wickham. Upset. That's how I am."

"You're not feeling well? How can I help?"

"No, no. You don't understand. It's that dead girl. And her husband."

"Edward Crane?"

"I just heard. This very minute. Found out what he sells. That so called medicine."

Lydia's words and the venom in her voice surprised Gracie. Her words didn't match Lydia's history of believing in implausible cures and nostrums. In past conversations Lydia had assured her listener of the virtues achieved through Phrenology, Hydropath, magnets and others of Lydia's new found "sciences."

"So called medicine, Lydia? Have you been taking it?"

"No, no, not me. But my sister—you remember my sister, Isabelle?"

Gracie had never met Lydia's sister but remembered hearing Lydia speak of her. It was easier to answer, "Yes."

"Well, I don't trust those so called tonics. Like Isabelle was taking. Oh!" Lydia's smooth cheeks flushed a becoming pink. "Oh, I'm sorry. I didn't mean tonics like you make from your herbs and all."

"I gathered you didn't, Lydia." Gracie remembered not to laugh at Lydia's confusion and further rattle her.

"Has your sister been taking Cranc's Golden Medicine Discovery? Is that why you're upset?"

"No, she wasn't taking that. But something just as bad. She became addicted to it."

"What was it?"

"Dr. Hostetter's Bitters."

Gracie briefly wondered why such remedies favored labels with 'doctor' in their name when licensed physicians condemned them as quackery. She recalled the American Medical Association had established a board to analyze quack remedies and enlighten the public. As a result, Hostetter's

Bitters was discovered to be almost fifty percent alcohol. She repeated this to Lydia.

"I knew it! I knew it. Poor Isabelle. Stumbling around like a common drunk. Almost ended her marriage when George threatened to have her committed."

"I am sorry, Lydia, but how does this relate to Mr. Crane?"

"I want you to do something about it."

"It?"

"The stuff he bottles. What he puts into it. Before more people like poor Isabelle become addicted and families are ruined."

Gracie had a brief fantasy of Lydia in her new found fervor against patent medicines joining the Temperance movement of primly dressed females to lead them like a strutting, angry peacock. Gracie herself could be criticized for enjoying a sherry with Ambrose. To Lydia she said, "I'm not sure there's a lot I can do about it, Lydia"

"But he's right here. At our hotel. You could march right over and forbid him, that's what you could do."

"No. I can't forbid him, as you say. But I can direct the attention of our state medical board to his product."

"Well then, do it!" and having righteously settled the matter in her own mind, Lydia flounced out of the office. Her faith in Miss Wickham's ability to solve problems appeared as firm as some of her less provable beliefs. Gracie sat shaking her head in amusement, as through the open door she watched Lydia almost knock against Hazel leading Annie O'Shea down the hall.

Twenty-Eight

Annie slid into the room as if her legs might not support her. She took the offered seat and looked around Miss Wickham's office.

The frightened girl had never before been in the large room with its examining table in the center and framed diplomas on the walls: Dr. Wickham's from the Deerfield Academy and Dartmouth Medical School, Miss Wickham's from the Glens Falls Academy and the certificate for the year she'd completed at Syracuse Medical College. Shelves on another wall held bottles of medicine, dried herbs and decoctions in small glass bottles with their cork stoppers; brass scales, measuring cylinders, a microscope on a lower shelf with various instruments on a counter top. A bookcase held her father's medical books and her own. Opposite that was the large desk Gracie returned to and pulled out her chair to sit and study Annie.

The nineteen-year-old girl looked nervous and patted her black curls where wisps escaped from hair pulled away from her face. The small scattering of freckles stood out against her paleness. "Thank you for seeing me, Miss Wickham." She stopped patting her hair and pulled her dark shawl closer. The contrast between Lydia Finley's assured presumptuousness and Annie's frightened meekness was striking.

"I'm here to help, Annie." Gracie lit a kerosene lamp on the desk. Outside, shadows from the back maple reached across the remaining snow. April days were lengthening and shadows

145

changing. She didn't want to rush Annie and sat quietly, waiting for her to begin.

Annie sniveled and sniffed, then wiped her nose with the back of her hand and said, "I had to tell you."

Gracie leaned forward encouragingly and said softly, "Tell me what?"

"About the husband."

"Mr. Crane?" How could Edward Crane have affected these two different women?

"I didn't know she'd been killed." Annie hung her head briefly. "Strangled, someone said."

"You didn't know she was dead when you told me about the blue dress?"

"No. I would've told you then. But I didn't know."

"Told me what?"

"I saw him."

"Her husband?"

"Sneaking into the hotel." Jenny took a deep breath as if to enable her to go on. "That morning."

"Tuesday morning?"

"Yes. Early it was. Sometimes I do breakfast. I had to be at work by six."

"And Mr. Crane was going into the hotel then?"

Jenny's body had been found by Moody Bedell at three in the morning. The time that rigor mortis set in indicated she had been killed around nine or ten o'clock Monday evening. Had the husband been out all night and lied about drinking in his room? Was this why he didn't know his partner had arrived Monday evening? Where was he coming from shortly before six o'clock Tuesday morning? And why? Had he been outside at nine the evening when Jenny was killed? She said none of this aloud.

"Did you speak to him?"

"No! I had just turned toward the hotel. I live where they let rooms in that house just south of the corner. He didn't see me from afar. I noticed him because he was acting sneaky-like and nobody was out and about. Then he started up the back stairs where the help comes in, not the front door for guests."

"Odd," Gracie said, more to herself than Annie.

"I didn't pay it no mind 'til I heard his wife was dead. Then I got scared 'cuz I wondered if he'd seen me after all and would hurt me next."

"You think he hurt his wife?"

"I saw him pulling on her arm. In the lobby, I mean. When his wife was talking to Sam Somerville."

"Have you told anyone else about this?"

"No." She shook her head vehemently. "I've been too scared."

"I'm glad you came to me, Annie. I think you'd best not tell anyone else just yet."

They sat in the soft glow of the lamp-lit room, each with their own thoughts. Annie's hands reached again to pull her shawl closer. Gracie had offered to see Jenny's husband about the keepsake of mourning jewelry. That would give her a chance to see if he was willing to explain his actions after saying he never left his room that evening. She'd need to tell Ambrose what she'd learned.

As if reading her thoughts, Annie asked, "What about you? Are you going to tell anyone?" She looked at Miss Wickham as if she was afraid of the answer.

Gracie held her father's gold watch in her hand as she adjusted the chain around her bony neck and thought. "Mr. Baldoon should know. You did nothing wrong and it's best that Mr. Baldoon knows what's going on with his guests."

"Wish I'd never seen anything," Annie said, forgetting how curious she'd been before.

"But you did, and you were right to come forward."

"I couldn't sleep last night. Knew you'd help me." Annie tried to go on and broke into shaking sobs. "Knew that...that you were the one to tell."

Gracie reached for Annie's hand and held it while she said, "You have nothing to fear, Annie. But I'm going to give you something to help you sleep." She considered what she had.

Chamomile wasn't strong enough. Same for nettle and elderberry. Aloud she said, "Hop, I think."

Annie looked startled. She was confused. Did Miss Wickham want her to jump?

Gracie saw her confusion and laughed. "Not you, Annie."

She stood up to look among the bottles on the shelf. "Humulus lupulus," she said, smiling. "Makes a good summer soup with other leafy vegetables. But we've a way to go to summer, haven't we?" Her voice was soothing as she turned and said, "I'm going to give you some hop tea that I want you to drink last thing tonight. To help you sleep. Do you by any chance have a hop-filled pillow?"

"A pillow filled with tea?" Would she ever understand these people?

Gracie laughed again. "No. Humulus lupulus is a plant well known for its calming effect on the nerves. Hop-filled pillows aid sleeplessness. I want you to drink the hop tea, two teaspoons in a cup of boiling water, and sleep on a hop filled pillow. I'll give you both."

Annie held her gifts as they walked down the hall together, Gracie's hand on her shoulder. "I'll just tell my housekeeper that I'll see you home. Then I'll explain what you saw to Mr. Baldoon and we'll see what he wants to do."

"I knew I'd feel better after I told you." Annie leaned into the tall woman like a small ship finding safe harbor.

Gracie's thoughts were on Galvin Swagger and how he'd immediately suspected Jenny's husband. No need to tell Annie what the partner said and worry her further. There were questions she wanted to ask the partner. He appeared to be the stronger personality, the businessman in the partnership, with Crane as the public front. As Lydia had said, they were in an odious business selling promises to gullible people. But were they killers?

Twenty-Nine

"Isn't it always the husband?" Ambrose said when she finished telling him Annie's secret.

"That's what Dr. Martin said too."

"What do you think, Gracie?"

"I'm curious about the time he was sneaking into the hotel, Ambrose. If he killed his wife earlier, what was he doing out until then? It makes no sense."

"Maybe he intended to move her body but it was gone when he went to look."

"Or maybe he was out looking for her when she didn't return." Gracie steepled her long fingers under her chin as she thought and went on. "He did admit he'd torn her dress and threw it in the hall when she didn't come in."

"Since the constable isn't here, it's time you found out what the husband has to say. Dr. Martin wants you to solve it, Gracie."

"Is he back?" Miss Wickham raised her light eyebrows and looked at Ambrose worriedly.

"Crane?" he asked.

"The coroner wants him held at the hotel until the constable returns."

Ambrose asked, "Where did you say he went?"

"The constable? Utica," she answered. "You told me. Some family business."

"I saw Crane and Swagger go into the dining room a short while ago. I can send word we'd like to see him in the office."

149

Without discussing it, they'd both refused to call Edward Crane *Doctor*.

"Yes, do that. I'll offer the mourning hair Margaret wants to make into a keepsake and see his reaction. It's possible he really did love his wife."

"Love her and beat her both?"

"Oh, Ambrose. Unfortunately there are men who do that, promising time and again they won't. Or justifying it somehow. His wife, his property." The very thing Susan railed against.

Ambrose stood to go, his large frame filling the door. Such a big man, she thought, and with no need to prove how big he was.

"I'd like to speak to Mr. Swagger as well...," she paused and added, "but separately. Unfortunately, they've had time to agree on a story. But I still have questions."

Edward Crane looked startled at seeing Miss Wickham sitting in the office. Apparently Ambrose hadn't told him she'd be there.

"You have something to say to me?" Jenny's husband raised his slim right hand to smooth his eyebrow and brought it down to adjust his floppy silk ascot. *He certainly acts like he's hiding something*, Gracie thought.

"Several things, actually," she said in a serious voice. "The coroner allowed me to have some strands of Jenny's hair in case you wanted a keepsake of mourning jewelry."

Edward swallowed as if relieved by this information. "Yes, yes, of course."

"There's a woman who makes such jewelry and would like to talk to you about it."

"Anything, anything," he looked around the office.

"Mr. Crane. You told us you were in your room the entire evening when your wife was killed. Drinking, I believe you said."

They both noticed beads of perspiration appear on his forehead as he once again raised his forefinger to his eyebrow. Only this time he touched his forehead and felt the dampness.

He reached into his waistcoat pocket, removed a handkerchief and patted his face. "That's right."

Ambrose spoke up. "Someone saw you coming in to the hotel early the next morning."

It was apparent Eddie Crane was doing some fast thinking as his eyes darted around the room and he rocked back on his heels.

"Well, when I woke she wasn't there and I went out looking for her."

"Why not alert the hotel authorities?" Ambrose said.

Gracie interrupted, saying, "The person who reported your actions wondered why you didn't use the front door for guests. Looked as if you were trying to come in without calling attention to yourself or the hour."

Unexpectedly Jenny's husband fell into the desk chair and threw his head on the top of the desk and began pounding it hard with both hands. "If she'd not gone out. Not gone out! None of this would have happened."

"And you went out, too, Mr. Crane," she said quietly.

He spun around quickly. "My wife was difficult. Young. Wouldn't listen."

"We're waiting for the constable to return to town to look into the matter. Until then the coroner asks that you not leave," Ambrose told him.

He looked up at their faces and didn't challenge what had been said.

"Where were you, if not in your room?"

"I was drinking for a while. That part's true." Gone was Edward Crane's theatrical affectation, his voice very low.

"And?"

"And I heard a man at the bar tell another about The Lavender House."

"You didn't know your partner was going to arrive?"

"Not then."

Gracie and Ambrose looked at each other. The Lavender House.

151

She had told Ambrose about her childhood adventure seeking the house up the road that she heard had so many cats. Miss Fanny English, who ran the house for fallen women, had graciously taken her into the kitchen to show her one lone cat. But the indignant little Gracie demanded to know why it was called a cat house if that's all there was. Her childish audacity could still bring high color to her cheeks when she thought about it.

Ambrose asked, "That's where you were coming from early in the morning? Not wanting to be seen?"

"Yes."

"That can be verified," Gracie told him.

"I have no intention of going there again," Crane said. "It was my anger at Jenny that drove me to go in the first place." He tried to pull a smile but couldn't. "You know. Let her worry about me for a change."

"There are other ways to deal with anger," Ambrose said.

"I didn't kill her if that's what you're implying."

Gracie said, "You returned to your room without knowing your partner had checked into the hotel?"

"I was at breakfast when he came up to me. I wasn't surprised to see him since I had left word I knew where Jenny was."

"Didn't he wonder why you and Jenny were gone all evening?"

"I told him Jenny never came back. We were both furious with her. Didn't know she was dead."

"Did you tell him where you'd been?" Ambrose asked.

Jenny's husband looked embarrassed. It was obvious who was the senior partner. "When he asked, yes."

"I have some questions for Mr. Swagger, too, about his activities that night," Gracie said.

"He wasn't with me. Galvin's all business." Eddie stood up, searching their faces to see if the interview was over.

"None the less, stay close to the hotel until the matter is settled," Ambrose informed him.

Realizing he was free to go, Eddie resumed his Dr. Crane voice. "I'll be in my room for the rest of the night," and with a nod to Miss Wickham he left the office.

"What do you think, Gracie?"

"I think Miss Fanny's establishment has been used before for an alibi. But I'll check with her to see about the time."

They walked out of the office together and found themselves facing Galvin Swagger. After learning of his partner's errant behavior, the large, rumpled man indicated his disgust and said, "The man acted foolishly but he has his strong points and is a magnetic speaker, essential in our business."

"I'd like to talk about your business, Mr. Swagger. Just what are the ingredients in your Golden Medical Discovery?" She had no intention of mentioning Lydia protests earlier, nor did she intend to ask the medical board to analyze the ingredients. She simply wanted to hear what he had to say. She couldn't help wondering what kind of conditions existed when this messy looking man mixed together his batch of syrup. He was simply unkempt. He pulled out his gold watch from his food-stained vest and looked at the time as if she was keeping him.

"That reminds me that your partner didn't know you were here until you met at breakfast," Gracie said. "When did you arrive?"

"I'm sure I arrived sometime after nine because the desk clerk told me both Dr. Crane and his wife had left the premises. I assumed they were together. There wasn't much to see at that time of night and after a short look around at what was outside the hotel I came inside. Knocked at their room several times and toward midnight gave up and settled in for the night."

"You got here before nine then?"

"By the time I found transportation from the station I believe it was after nine," he said. His eyes narrowed when he added, "You certainly aren't suggesting I came here with the intent of killing the golden egg, so to speak?"

"I'm not suggesting anything, Mr. Swagger." To describe Jenny as the golden egg in a scheme to sell their syrup annoyed her.

"Good night to both of you then," and with a nod, Swagger shuffled off.

"He' didn't want to talk about what he puts in his syrup, did he, Gracie?"

"But he wanted us to know he arrived at a time when Jenny and her husband were both missing," she answered. She thought about the husband's answer for his whereabouts that evening and said, "I'll go see Miss Fanny first thing tomorrow."

"Let me drive you."

At that moment they saw the stagecoach driver enter and walk to the front desk to announce the river drive was coming. It would reach The Glen by tomorrow.

Thirty

When the rider came with word to shut down for the drive, Tom Stockton had things he had to attend to. All but the driving crew for Nexus North needed to be paid off and accounts from the company store or "van" had to be adjusted. Throughout the winter men could get simple necessaries like socks and tobacco. Most lumberjacks seldom kept a record of their purchases and trusted the company's honesty. Tom had little intention of shortchanging his men for supplies although they all knew some logging firms cut into the men's profits this way.

Once word came to open his skidway, Tom walked quickly to tell the first of the two dam keepers.

"Pull away the upright planks at the crib dam holding back the water," he ordered.

Men not busy gathering their belongings watched as Tom waited with his timepiece to give the next order. After a flow of twenty to thirty minutes, the massive log boom, secured with thick hand-forged chains, would be lifted by the second dam keeper. Then the logs could join the roaring water and be on their way with the men chasing after them.

In spite of his long-standing and bitter feelings toward his river boss, John Dillon, Tom Stockton recognized the genius of the plan that fed the stored Adirondack water from streams and brooks, ponds and lakes, and smaller rivers. After the logs were on their way, down, down, tumbling down into the Hudson carrying the spruce and hemlock, the dams would be closed to store water for later release.

Tom gladly left camp, anxious to be on his way. Still, he felt uneasy about the written message he received earlier from Jacques.

Meet me when the drive reaches The Glen.

Why? Tom would be there anyway following the drive. Why the change in plans? The original idea was to meet in Glens Falls to share the money and now Tom wondered what it meant to meet sooner. He wouldn't know how much the bonus was until the logs were counted in Glens Falls.

He'd had all winter to regret going along with the crazy scheme. And there were other things bothering Tom. The State Commission formed two years ago was one. They were looking into broader state ownership of timber lands. What did 'a park' mean? Would the state buy and own land for fools and fops who talked about the joys of nature? Let them spend long winter months with below zero temperatures. Chop at frozen water and carry it before it froze again. A bunch of loony dreamers who didn't understand how fickle nature could be. Deprive men who were only trying to earn a living just so city slickers could have a summer playground?

Maybe no one was paying attention to that kind of talk but Tom listened and prided himself about knowing what went on. And another thing. He'd seen a team loaded with logs four inches and less in diameter. Brown sticks they were! He wasn't allowed to cut spruce like that. Those four-inch "straws" were going to end up as paper.

More pulp mills were being built. Pulp for paper. The writing was on the wall. He smiled wryly at his own joke. The end of lumbering as he knew it. One more reason to get out of this business.

And now the damn weather. Middle of April and snow falling on him as his men pushed off on their cold, wet journey. Heavy, wet stuff that would add to the frothy water. But meanwhile it was soaking him. His dark beard had turned white with snowflakes.

If he lived long enough, he mused, there'd be a day when his beard would be permanently white. If he lived that long… Old men weren't found lumbering or on the river drive. They were crippled or dead. No matter what new idea, schemes, or plans anyone came up with, Tom was finished with this one. Finished with lumbering forever. This would be his last drive.

Thirty-One

Like distant rumbling thunder, the voices of the gathered crowd at The Glen could be heard before Ambrose and the three women rounded the bend and saw the scene. Lumberjacks, joyously rushing to meet family members in arriving buckboards, trampled mud from the river's edge into the sandy soil of scarred and worn wagon tracks. Shouted greetings and words of welcome muted the sound of bubbling water spilling over stranded boulders off shore. Hundreds of thousands of herded logs nestled in slow water beyond the nearby wooden bridge, bobbing quietly.

River men with their ever-present pipes increased the smoke filled air already thick from cooking food and a blazing fire. The big tent where they slept in their clothes, packed in like canned sardines, was already set up a short distance from the Gilchrist house at The Glen. Over the years meeting the river drivers had become a special treat, a yearly ritual for local people who marked it as the end of winter.

The drive's cook and his helper had prepared the deep hole for the bean-hole-beans and built the fire the previous night so the coals would be ready. Squealing children chased each other, and barking dogs added to the multitude of loud voices. Bean-hole-beans from the huge kettle were a favorite of the children who got to taste them, along with a chance to drink from men's tin cups the coffee and tea not always allowed at home. Fruit pies, pickled eggs, cookies, ham and steak slices, everything the hungry men ate was shared with those who came out to meet them.

Sunset was still two hours off when Gracie and Ambrose arrived. High above the low-lying cooking smoke the sky was a brilliant banner of color, largely ignored by those caught up in more exciting earthbound activities. Ragged ribbons of clouds, like paper torn and scattered by a child using pinks and patches of blue, stretched across the sky. A reflecting sun sent bands of gold through the streaks of color, and the surrounding dark mountains sheltered the river's edge gathering.

Ambrose tied the horse to a sapling in the ash grove and helped the women alight from his buckboard. Margaret rushed to the big Gilchrist house eager to find her sister Fiona, and tell her about the mourning jewelry she was making for Jenny's husband.

Gracie wondered aloud if the Somervilles had arrived looking for Paddy. She scanned the crowd for a sight of Lewis LaPierre and called out to Ambrose when she thought she saw him.

"Look, Ambrose! Isn't that Jenny's brother? He must be searching for men he knew at the logging camp."

"Hardly recognize him," Ambrose said. "But for that big coat he wears. Looks like he cleaned up. Shaved, too."

"You'd think he'd want to leave his beard to look older. Most boys do."

"Maybe he's aware it's not the fashion these days."

She smiled at him. "Is that why you wanted to have a barber at the hotel? More men have given up beards?"

"Here, let me carry that for you," Ambrose said and took the large basket from Hazel's hands. They followed Gracie picking her way through blankets set on the ground, greeting neighbors and lumbermen she knew. It wasn't long before Hazel said she'd find them later and left to join Margaret and Fiona.

"There's John Dillon—over there," Ambrose said. "Is that his wife with him? Your friend?"

She waved in greeting. "Yes, that's Addie Dillon."

Ambrose started toward them when Gracie stopped him with a hand on his arm. "Wait, Ambrose. Look. Lewis has found someone." She'd turned again to look at Jenny's brother. "See. It must be someone he knows from the camp."

Ambrose stopped and stared. "Didn't you tell me Lewis LaPierre had been at Newtown camp? The camp Paddy worked at?" he asked.

"Yes."

"Well, Jenny's brother is talking to the forester at Nexus North. I met him when John took me to see the skidways. Tom something."

"That's Tom Stockton? I haven't seen him in ages."

"Look, they're walking away." Ambrose turned to her. "Why do I get the feeling they don't want to be noticed by this crowd."

"How would Jenny's brother know Tom Stockton from Nexus North?" she wondered aloud.

"I thought we were going to find out if Paddy knew him from Newtown camp?"

"Yes, but where is Paddy?" She searched the crowd with her eyes before saying, "Let's find Kate and Sam. That's how we'll find Paddy and see if he knows Lewis."

As they started through gathered groups of people they heard music and singing coming from the river's edge. A group surrounded the man playing the fiddle while a lumberjack sang out: "Come all you true shanty boys wherever you be, Give your attention and listen to me." As they grew closer others who knew the song clapped and shouted out the chorus "So merry, so merry, so merry are we...high derry, low derry, low derry down dee."

Fearing Gracie would be trampled as more closed in, Ambrose touched her elbow. She looked up at him, smiled and nodded she was ready to move away. They picked their way to a cleared space and spied the Somerville family they intended to join. Kate Somerville greeted them as they approached, shaking out her bonnet and retying it. The bloom of her health was back. "We just got here. Have you seen Paddy? You know my mother? Robbie? Sam? Everybody?"

Gracie began to introduce Ambrose again, but he reminded them they'd met at sugaring time. Just then Paddy pushed through a cluster of people and burst upon them, picking up Kate and swinging her off her feet as he hugged her.

"And this is Tebo," he said when he set her down and introduced everyone to his new friend.

For a few moments there was excited back slapping and exchanged greetings. Once they settled to eat, Paddy took over, full of river news. He began telling of the man they'd lost on the drive and how he'd finally gotten a turn in the jam boat and his use of dynamite.

As if he knew it was expected of him, Tebo told of Paddy's daring rescue when he jumped on the back of the log of a trapped driver. This gave Paddy the chance to expand on each story and let Sam know what he'd missed. Sam, finally getting a chance to get in a word when Paddy had his mouth full, quietly asked if Paddy remembered someone at camp named Lewis LaPierre.

Gracie hadn't expected the question so soon. And that it came from Sam. She'd planned on finding Lewis to ask if he'd yet met any of the men from Paddy's camp, Newtown logging. Perhaps ask Lewis to join them. Paddy's answer stunned her.

"Yeah," he said. "That's the name of the kid who hung himself and nearly burned down the cookhouse at camp." Slurping coffee from his tin cup and wiping his mouth with the back of his hand he asked, "Right, Tebo?"

He turned away from Tebo to look at his family. "You all heard about the fire?" Paddy asked. "Didn't I write you that, Kate? The damn cold saved us or we'd have lost it all."

Kate nodded in bewilderment as if this was the first she'd heard of it.

Tebo continued to eat his bean hole beans as he, too, nodded, seemingly unaware of the changed faces staring at him and Paddy. Ambrose and Gracie had stopped eating, trying to take in what they had heard and a shocked silence followed, as if all the voices of the crowd around them had stopped suddenly, waiting.

"But..." Gracie stammered, "...he's here." She regretted the words as soon as she uttered them. She was troubled by the sudden turn of events and what she might have added to them. Was this the time and place for a confrontation?

Sam finally found his voice and said, "Then who's that saying he's Lewis LaPierre?"

Paddy said, "What are you talking about?"

"Someone calling himself Lewis LaPierre is here," Ambrose said.

"What? What!" Paddy confused eyes looked at them incredulously as he shook his head. "Can't be! The kid hung himself last winter. Tebo? Sam? You remember him? Sam?"

A shaken Sam answered, "No. I wasn't there long enough."

Tebo looked from face to face as it dawned on him that something was amiss and looked to Paddy for direction. Paddy said belligerently, "Hold on." He stood up and threw down his tin cup as if it was a gauntlet. "Let's go find this so called Lewis LaPierre and see what he has to say for himself."

At the back of the Gilchrist House beside a group of sheltering balsam he thought concealed them, Jacques Girard pulled the marking hammer from his deep coat pocket.

"Why the hell did you bring that here?" Tom's gimlet eyes darkened.

"You didn't think I would leave it behind, did you?"

"This was a stupid idea to meet here. I won't know until we get to Glens Falls how much we made."

Ignoring his protest, Jacques smirked, "It's got to be more than last year, Tom Stockton. I marked enough logs to earn you a good bonus." He smiled again and corrected himself. "Us, a good bonus." He fingered the raised metal head on its wooden arm and gleefully went on.

"Dumb to saw off the marks on the logs. They get suspicious when they find the pieces left behind. This is fool proof."

Once he had convinced Tom that he could get away with it, Jacques had gone on to urge Tom to have the Nexus blacksmith make the punch mark he now fingered.

He'd assured Tom it was a simple plan and eagerly promised, "I'll take all the risk." All Tom had to do once the punch mark was made was meet him in Glens Falls. "I'll take my reward when you get the bonus for more logs."

Only now Jacques was here and Tom was beginning to ask questions. Why Jacques had left Newtown's camp and hadn't gone on the drive. Why Jacques sent word he'd meet Tom at The Glen. Tom kept looking around expecting to see someone approach.

Jacques started explaining why he was there, looking very different with his beard gone.

"What went wrong?" a troubled Tom Stockton asked.

"This kid at Newtown loggers followed me one night. Caught me changing the logs. *Mon dieu!* The whole plan upended! He had to be silenced!"

Tom shook his head in dismay.

"Made it look like a suicide. Helped fight the fire that night. Then eventually got out of there." He paused to grin. "I'd already changed plenty of markings. Why not start over with a new name? He wasn't gonna use it any more. I found work 'til I could get word to you. Explain it all, you know?"

Tom stepped away. Holy mother! Jacques had killed the kid! Tom shuddered with fear. He could feel the noose himself. The hangmen's halter.

Thirty-Two

Everyone stood up at once, upsetting the blanket and picnic things. Gracie froze in place, as if by not moving she could stop time and gather together what she knew so far, recalling the few scraps Jenny had told about her brother. The first surprise came when the men at the boarding house told of his gambling. And then why he'd missed work. There was the first meeting in her home when Lewis came with Moody to hear about Jenny and how he'd looked when he heard she was dead. His reaction upon meeting Jenny's husband. All the while everyone believing this man was Jenny Crane's brother.

Who was he and why did he say he was Lewis LaPierre? None of it made any sense and now Paddy was spoiling for a fight.

"Where is he?" Paddy demanded.

She felt as if a thousand faces were looking at her and echoing Paddy's words. She pointed through the crowd to where she had seen Lewis walking back of the Gilchrist house. "Paddy should not go alone," she cautioned, then felt foolish as her face flamed, for she could see his brothers and Tebo had no intention of letting that happen.

Ambrose looked at her and said, "If you're thinking of following, you're not going alone." Apparently the interested onlookers agreed.

They all trailed in the cleared path Paddy made by his saying loudly, "Out of my way." Paddy's known temper and history of an eagerness to settle disputes with his fists foretold an ugly confrontation that alerted more people. Gracie had an image of a swarm of bees collecting, emigrating with a queen bee. Only in this case the dense, moving crowd was being led by an angry hornet named Paddy Somerville. The sound of stomping boots and rising voices of on-lookers who joined in, sensing a fight and not wanting to miss the excitement, should have alerted Tom Stockton.

But the two men standing by the sheltering balsams seemed to be arguing and unaware of those bearing down on them. Gracie was almost on Sam's heels when she heard Paddy shout, "Who says he's Lewis LaPierre?"

Jacques looked around, quickly taking in the angry faces, his eyes seeking a route of escape. Seeing none, he panicked and raised the marking hammer with his simian-like long right arm as if to ward off anyone who thought of coming closer.

Tom Stockton looked out at what had become a mob scene of loud voices led by Paddy. He turned back to see a crazed Jacques dancing in place and waving the marking hammer. "No!" Tom screamed. He reached out, attempting to wrest what was now a deadly weapon from his conspirator's hands. Jacques pulled aside and stepped back with manic strength and swung with all his might, striking a heavy blow to Tom's head. A blow that had been intended for Paddy. Tebo screamed something in French.

Startled by the scream, Jacques looked down and saw the fallen Tom Stockton. Ambrose seized the moment to grab the raised punch mark just as Paddy leapt and tackled the imposter. It happened in a rush of confusing seconds. Paddy's lunge grounded his victim into the trampled earth. Face up in the mud, Paddy flipped him over so he could twist his arms behind his back to be quickly held by Sam and Tebo. Paddy propped the imposter, twisting, grunting and swearing, to a sitting position and screamed in his face, "Who are you?"

In the noisy melee, the fallen man was ignored as the mass of Paddy's audience pressed closer to hear the answer. Gracie knelt beside Tom's prostrate form to check his vital signs and looked up at the gathered crowd watching and waiting for answers. She shook her head and said in a low voice, "He's dead." Gracie looked at the cowering figure who'd called himself Lewis LaPierre, muddy and sweaty from the scuffle, to see if he'd heard her.

"It was an accident," Jacques whined, gasping for breath, taking in the crowd of angry faces looking down on him.

Paddy shouted in his face. "Was it an accident, a suicide or murder that killed the real Lewis LaPierre?" He squatted in front of the restrained man, scanning the muddied face and suddenly blurted, "Jesus! It's Jacques! Jacques Girard! You bastard! You shaved your beard, but it's you!" and with that Paddy cuffed him on the side of the head.

Ambrose, still holding the marking hammer said, "None of that!" in a voice that echoed his years as a military man.

Gracie came up beside Ambrose and said to Paddy, "There's been enough violence."

Sam pointed at Jacques Girard and in the loudest voice anyone ever heard Sam use, said, "Then he must be the one who killed Jenny. She'd know he wasn't her brother."

"Yeah, yeah..." Voices from the standing crowd agreed, some shaking their fists. Gracie looked at Sam. His accusation was so quick. Why? Was it relief from the fears he surely had when he'd been under suspicion? But if this wasn't Lewis LaPierre, it was true that Jenny would have exposed him.

"You killed her," voices shouted, overcoming Jacques' denials.

"Murderer!" others shouted, looking down at the fallen body of Tom Stockton.

Gracie took several steps away from the imposter and said to Ambrose. "He should be taken to the sheriff in Lake George." She turned and explained to the hardened faces of the curious who now sought vengeance, "The constable is away. But the sheriff there can take care of this."

Paddy dragged Jacques to his feet. Ambrose ordered that the body of Tom Stockton be brought with them and offered his buckboard to go to the Lake George jail, some twelve miles away.

With Tebo and Ambrose following, Paddy started to lead his prisoner away. Ambrose turned back to search for her in the crowd of faces and finding her said, "I'll return for you, Gracie." She nodded and watched Robbie and Sam carry the dead Tom Stockton as Paddy pushed Jacques stumbling through the parted crowd.

The formerly festive atmosphere was gone. People began gathering up their things to leave, full of the shocking news they would talk about for days and spread to any who hadn't joined them at The Glen. Gracie turned around to walk to the Gilchrist house to tell Hazel and the others what had happened outside. She would wait there for Ambrose to return.

The women had rushed to the windows of the Gilchrist's wide porch when they heard the commotion outside. After listening to all they missed, Hazel shook her head and said, "He couldn't risk her telling he wasn't her brother, could he? That's why he killed Jenny."

Gracie said, "It would seem so. But he was vehement in his denials."

Back in the kitchen Margaret reached for one of Fiona's fresh doughnuts and said, "Well, he's safely put away in jail. Won't be killing anyone now."

Fiona brought Miss Wickham a cup of tea and set it in front of her. "Did you get anything at all to eat?"

"A little. But this will be fine." She sat at the round table, silently going over the sudden turn of events. The different men she had suspected. She'd always thought the murderer was someone Jenny had known since there was no evidence of a struggle. Wouldn't she have struggled against the imposter claiming to be her brother? Did she have time?

Margaret gushed on happily that now that Edward Crane wouldn't be going to jail he could still buy her mourning jewelry.

Hazel interrupted sharply, "If the man is free to leave now, you'd best hurry up and get it done," which set Margaret pacing and looking out the window for Ambrose to return.

Thirty-Three

The next morning Gracie met Ambrose in his office as he finished eating his usual large breakfast of sausage and eggs and steaming corn muffins. They hadn't had a chance to talk on the way home last night because Hazel and Margaret had traveled back with them. Margaret had much to say and told a scowling Hazel how she'd always suspected something about that brother.

"Got only a glimpse of him that time you sent me off to get me out of the house." She glanced accusingly at Hazel as she spoke to Miss Wickham. "If I'd been able to study him I could have told you he was at Nexus when I was cook that winter. Friendly with Tom Stockton. Course he wore a beard then."

Hazel replied gruffly. "Well you didn't study him and you didn't tell us who he really was, so I imagine that's so." Any further talk had ended until they arrived home and said their good-nights.

Ambrose requested a waitress to bring coffee for Miss Wickham. While they waited she glanced at the top of his desk. Ambrose had the marking hammer he'd taken from the imposter Jacques Girard resting there on the desk, and she lifted it to examine it more closely.

He watched her and after a few moments said, "I should have given it to the sheriff but with all the commotion and the effort to keep Paddy from beating the stuffing out of that imposter, I walked away with it." He sipped his coffee and said, "I'll see that he gets it or show it to Jeremiah when he returns."

169

"I don't think he intended to kill Tom," she said unexpectedly.

"Lewis? I mean Jacques Girard?"

She smiled, "It does take getting used to, doesn't it?"

Ambrose wiped his mouth with the large white napkin. "Well, Paddy's sure the imposter killed the real Lewis LaPierre at Newtown's logging camp."

"It looks that way if he assumed his identity. But why do that? Because the boy hadn't been there long and few people knew him? And what was the connection the imposter had with Tom Stockton?"

She kept studying the punch mark she had seen before in the boarding house bedroom hidden under the bed. Why hide it? It didn't match any of the lumber companies who were part of the river drive. Why did he take it to The Glen? To show Tom Stockton? Had he intended all along to kill Tom? But why? How did they know each other?

She let out a gasp of understanding as she fingered the upraised metal slash mark that ran from the top right to bottom left.

"Ambrose! Tom Stockton was the jobber for Nexus not Newtown loggers."

Ambrose said, "Dillon's wife last night. She must have heard what happened to Tom. You said she knew him?"

Gracie went on thinking aloud. "Ambrose, listen. Now we know Jacques Girard worked at Newtown when he killed Jenny's brother, but Margaret remembers him with Tom Stockton when she was cook at Nexus North!" Her voice rose with excitement. "And Newtown sends its logs down with the big N stamped into each end of its logs."

"What's your point, Gracie?"

She held up the marking hammer and ran her finger against the metal slash mark. "Look, Ambrose. If you joined the N. Here..." she reached over and picked up a pencil and paper and began drawing. "Look. I've just changed the N into the symbol for Nexus." She turned the paper around so he could see the crude butterfly she made by drawing a slash from one point of

170

the N to another. "Simple, wasn't it? With this marker, Newtown logs suddenly become logs belonging to Nexus North."

"So that was their game."

"Once the logs are marked and stored in the skidway, no one would look to see if the marking was changed. Unless Jenny's brother had somehow discovered it."

She sat thoughtfully and looked up inquiringly to ask, "But why if Otis Andrus owns both camps?"

"There's always a bonus involved. Dillon told me that when I was with him, Gracie."

"Tom must have been desperate to go along with that," she said softly. "To send down Newtown's logs as his own!"

"You think Jenny's brother, the real Lewis LaPierre, caught this man changing the marks at Newtown's camp after they were stored in the skidway? That's why he killed him? To shut him up? Tried to make it look like a suicide?"

When she didn't answer, Ambrose went on. "Odd he took the chance to be seen at The Glen where someone could recognize him."

"You were the one, Ambrose, who recognized it was Tom Stockton he was talking to. You'd seen Tom recently."

"Which didn't make sense if this fellow had worked at Newtown's camp."

"Without his beard, Paddy didn't recognize him right away," Gracie said.

"And if Paddy hadn't seen him, identified him...." Ambrose didn't finish his sentence, just sat looking at her, stunned at the deception that almost succeeded.

"It explains the connection with Tom Stockton at least," she finished for him. She fingered the marking hammer as she added, "They had to have hatched this plan before Jacques Girard went to work at Newtown so he could change the markings to Nexus."

"Pretty risky, I'd say," Ambrose shook his head in wonderment.

Gracie nodded and Ambrose continued, "And why he killed Jenny even if he denies it. Who else could have done it?"

"Yes, who?" she answered.

Thirty-Four

Ambrose left his office with Gracie in time to see Galvin Swagger and his partner leaving the dining room and coming toward them in the hotel lobby.

Edward Crane spoke first. "We heard. My wife's killer's been found. That young man wasn't her brother after all?" He looked smug as he added ingratiatingly, "Since I never met the real Lewis LaPierre..." He let the sentence end there as if it exonerated him from any responsibility. His theatrical pose was back as he said to Ambrose, "I am no longer to be detained here, then?"

Ambrose looked at Gracie before he said, "Not as far as I'm concerned."

"Then we'll arrange for transportation to North Creek. You have a train schedule here?" As if he could still be accused of something, Crane fingered his ascot as he spoke, avoiding looking directly at their eyes.

Ambrose turned back to the front desk and reached behind it to hand him a train schedule.

Standing beside his partner, Swagger used a toothpick to remove remnants of his breakfast that had not spilled on his vest. "We'll read it while the barber cleans us up, Eddie." He smiled benignly on them and shambled off, his salt and pepper shock of hair looking as if it hadn't yet been combed. He conveyed an image of a pleasant but messy man who could use a haircut as well as a shave.

173

Crane scowled at his partner's use of the nickname but followed as Swagger shambled ahead to the barber's shop set up for the hotel's clients next to Ambrose's office.

"Something about those two still bother you, Gracie?"

"Yes."

Annie was heading toward the dining room with a tray of clean silverware. "I think I'll have a word with Annie." She explained to Ambrose, "She's been nervous about Jenny's husband. Afraid he might harm her. I'm sure she's heard about Jacques Girard by now, but I'll take a minute to reassure her they're leaving."

After talking with the young waitress who seemed relieved with word that the two men from Saratoga would soon be gone, Gracie decided to walk over to the general store. Perhaps the owner might remember something more about Jenny's visit there the night she was killed. Had anyone else come in at the time? Had he seen anyone outside when Jenny left? But Mr. Austin repeated the same story he'd given before and there was nothing new to learn from him about that night.

Ambrose was standing behind the registration desk when she returned to the hotel and told him, "Annie's feeling better. Relieved to know Mr. Crane is leaving the building for good."

"I'll be getting their bill together. They're upstairs packing." Ambrose turned and left for his office.

Something bothered Gracie about their leaving and she thought again of their arrivals. She stepped to where Ambrose had gotten the train schedule, found another and studied it. Why hadn't she thought of this before? She looked up, her mind racing, and noticed the barber in the doorway of his new shop.

He was looking at the people passing through the lobby. The name "Junior" didn't seem to fit an elderly, white-haired man. He smiled at her in a friendly manner which encouraged her to see if he might reveal anything about the partners who'd gone in for a shave.

She approached the barber with a smile. "I hope you gave that rumpled man a needed haircut along with his shave." She

174

considered how to ask what they might have been talking about.

Junior chuckled at her remark. "No, but for just a shave he's a big tipper. Heard them talking about the wife's killer. He was found?"

"That's what people believe," she said wondering what else they might have said.

"He'll need a lawyer."

Gracie looked puzzled and said, "Who?"

"That imposter they were talking about." Junior added with a smile, "Maybe the pretty one will represent him."

"The pretty one?" an amused Gracie asked.

"Not the one with all that wild hair for sure," Junior said. "Can't see him as a lawyer, but the other one, maybe."

Startled by his assumption, she asked, "Why would you say that?"

"Isn't he a lawyer?"

"No. But what made you think he was?"

"Looked like legal paper folded inside his jacket. Saw it when I hung it up to shave him."

"Legal paper?" She was confused for a minute. She took a deep breath and struggled to keep her voice even. "Did it look like a deed?"

"Could be." The barber scratched his head as if it helped him think. "Folded. I didn't see it up close."

"Thank you." With this new information she hurried back to Ambrose at his office desk to tell him what the barber said. "Ambrose!" Talking as much to herself as to him. "If it is the deed to the farm that Jenny had with her, how did the husband get it? From Jenny's room before we searched there? Does his partner know he has it?"

Ambrose's expression changed from surprise to a grim mask. "I'll have both into the office to settle the bill. You can ask them then," he assured her. "Let me take care of something first. I'd like someone to back me up if it's needed." When he returned Gracie saw the bar bouncer was not far from the office door.

While they waited for Jenny's husband and his partner to return to settle the bill, Gracie explained what she suspected. She'd just finished when the partners entered and showed no surprise at seeing Miss Wickham sitting there.

One look at the proprietor's face and Crane asked nervously, "Is there a problem with the account?"

"Well, there is a problem," Ambrose answered.

Gracie stood to say, "We never found the deed to the farm that Jenny was bringing to her brother."

"What does that have to do with us?" Swagger asked.

"Perhaps you'd better ask your partner," she said.

He looked at Eddie and his avuncular manner vanished as he irritably said, "Do you know what she's talking about?"

Nervously, Jenny's husband looked at him and then the others as if deciding something.

Swagger asked, "Are you going to give us our bill or do we walk out of here now without paying?" He waved a beefy arm to take in the room. "I'm getting tired of all the badgering in this neck of the woods."

"You're not going anywhere at the moment, Swagger," said Ambrose. He came from behind his desk and closed the door as he stood in front of it, the hotel help now outside the door. "You were saying, Gracie?"

"I'd like to see the legal paper Mr. Crane has with him. Have you seen it, Mr. Swagger?"

With an exasperated gesture Crane reached inside his jacket and pulled out the deed, holding it up. His voice trembled as he explained, "I found it in our room. She must have left it there. I've been carrying it with me since for safe keeping."

His voice was on the edge of sobbing when he continued, "I wasn't even around when she was killed."

Swagger rasped. "Neither was I."

Gracie turned to Galvin Swagger. "When *did* you get here?" Gracie asked. "You said you arrived here when Mr. and Mrs. Crane were both out." She held up a train schedule. "But the train schedule for Monday night indicates the last train pulled in to North Creek a few minutes after seven, giving you time to arrive here earlier than you said you did."

It dawned on Eddie what she was implying and he looked at his partner with a shocked expression and open mouth, as if the words he started to say had frozen there.

Looking puzzled, he said in a bewildered voice to his partner, "But you always liked her."

Gracie asked again, "How did the deed she always kept with her get left in her room?"

Swagger pointed at his partner, grabbing the deed out of his hands. "He's the one knocked her around. Ask him why she wanted to get away."

Shocked by his partner's accusation he whined, "I only disciplined her. She could be difficult."

"I came here to protect her from you. All I did was—" Swagger swayed angrily. "I don't like this. Any of it. Get hold of yourself, Eddie. No one can prove anything." He held the deed against his chest as if defending it and glared at Miss Wickham.

Gracie confronted him. "She didn't want to return to Saratoga, did she? That farm inheritance was her ticket out to a better life. Away from you two." Eddie flinched from her words but Swagger continued to glare at Gracie as she went on. "How did the deed come to be in her room? Who took it from her? Who put it there?"

Swagger snarled at her. "Must have been Eddie."

"Me?" Eddie Crane looked as if he'd been hit. "You! You had to have taken it from Jenny! I didn't know when you arrived. You got into the room I left open for her!"

Staring in disbelief at his partner, Crane shouted, "You told me to keep it safe when I showed it to you. Not to throw it away." He added, "You were setting me up for this!"

"He says he went to the cat house," Swagger retaliated. "Yeah, but after he killed her."

"No. I've had word from Lavender House as to the time he spent there." Gracie spoke to Swagger. "We've learned where he was at the time his wife died. It couldn't have been him."

Surprised by her challenge, Galvin Swagger came closer to his partner's face and began yelling at him, venting his rage. "She wouldn't listen! Wouldn't come back to you...to the hotel." He swung around and pointed at Miss Wickham. "Said she was going to your house. Regular little busy body, aren't you? Helping our Jenny leave us."

Ambrose remained blocking the closed door, grimly facing the two men as he said, "You strangled her, Swagger, and took the deed."

Ignoring the accusation, Swagger said, "I should have burned it immediately." He threw the deed on the desk. "Doing you a favor, Eddie. It's all yours now. Stupid farm girl. Didn't know when she was better off."

"You killed my Jenny?" Not willing to believe the accusations he'd just made against his partner, Jenny's husband leaned against the desk and sobbed. Gracie wondered whether he was crying over his wife or his partner's betrayal.

"Don't be so shocked, Eddie," Swagger sneered. "How many times did you come close to killing her yourself? Knocking her around? It was an accident when we struggled with the deed."

Gracie spoke up. "I think not, Mr. Swagger. There was no evidence of a struggle. Jenny was strangled quickly by someone she knew with strong hands." She looked at Swagger's large hands. "Someone angry."

"If she'd just given up the deed," he grumbled to himself collapsing in the chair behind Ambrose's desk.

"Enough!" Ambrose said sternly. "We'll be taking you, Mr. Swagger, to the jail in Lake George." He looked at his weeping partner and with no attempt to hide his disgust said, "And you can stay here and take care of the bill."

Ambrose rapped on the door and the bar bouncer came in and took Swagger's arm. Ambrose followed the two men out to the lobby then turned back to look at Gracie standing in the open doorway. He shook his head. "I'll see you when I get back," he said. "We'll talk then."

Thirty-Five

The lengthening spring days meant Ambrose returned from Lake George before dark, pleased to see his hotel's gas lights already lighting up the surrounding evening sky. His broad smile revealed his pleasure at seeing Gracie waiting for him in the lobby. He'd promised they would have a special dinner when he got back and his good humor indicated it looked to be a celebration.

He offered his arm, telling her about his short journey to the Lake George jail, adding, "Swagger's denying everything. Accusing his partner of taking the deed before Jenny left from Saratoga." He shook his head, "Changes his story when he thinks of something new."

She walked with him into the dining room where he held a chair for her. "Thank you, Ambrose." Seated she said, "Not very smart of Crane to have it in his pocket, but he didn't expect it to be damning evidence. And Swagger, a pack rat who couldn't bear to throw anything away, for all his smarts didn't think of it as evidence that would prove his undoing."

Ambrose chuckled at her description of the slovenly man now locked up in the Lake George jail, then asked, "I've been wondering. Crane accused his partner of setting him up to be the one suspected of killing his wife. Do you think that's the case?"

Gracie gazed off, giving his question some thought. "Perhaps. He's certainly a shrewd man. I think it's more likely Swagger realized the husband could make a claim on the property, but he couldn't. By leaving the deed in the room for Jenny's husband to find—and remember Crane said Swagger told him to hang on to it—my guess is that he thought they could eventually profit from the farm's sale."

"Did Crane leave?"

"Yes. Checked out while you were in Lake George."

"They would have both left, Gracie, if you hadn't gone over and talked to my barber."

"That was a piece of luck. Galvin Swagger might have gotten away with Jenny's murder."

"It was more than luck you thought to check the train schedule for Monday night. There was no way he could have come in later."

"Unless he was delayed in North Creek."

"He wasn't. He came in on the regular stage drop. I checked with the desk clerk before I took him to the sheriff."

"And Jacques Girard would have been blamed."

"That man's not what you would call lily white, Gracie."

They were seated at the table Ambrose usually chose in a far corner where he could see the entire dining room from his vantage point. He waved away the menus Annie offered. "No need, Annie," he told her. "I left our order in the kitchen."

Annie blushed and mumbled an excuse and left them.

"No, Ambrose, you're right. The imposter isn't lily white if he did away with Jenny's brother as we suspect. But even if we can't prove that, he'll be punished for killing Tom Stockton."

"He tried to blame it all on Stockton, you know. On our way to the jail, he rambled on. Said everything was Tom's idea."

"Andrus Otis owns both companies but the bonus goes to those who send down the most logs," she mused. "Tom had to be desperate to go along with that."

"It was a clever plan that almost succeeded. But stupid of the Frenchy to show up at The Glen where someone would recognize him."

"But he was clean shaven. Paddy didn't recognize him immediately, remember?"

She thought about the scheme the two at Nexus North had put together and reminded Ambrose, "When they used to paint their mark on the logs, some unsavory characters would saw the ends off, paint their own symbol and put the logs back in the water." She shook her head slightly as if to dismiss the idea. "The marking hammer was supposed to take care of that problem." She smiled and said, "But someone will always try..." She was interrupted by gas lamps in the room sputtering, then momentarily strengthened again, casting a soft light throughout the room.

Just then a smiling Annie came to the table to bring the first course of oysters. Ambrose nodded at Annie as he accepted them and said to Gracie, "Came in from Boston on the noon train."

"What will happen to Crane now?" she wondered aloud as she watched Ambrose nod again to dismiss Annie.

"I have no idea. But without his partner to make the syrup they sold, I would assume he's out of business." He picked up his fork and speared his first oyster.

"I wonder..." She told him about Lydia's unexpected visit demanding something be done about Galvin Swagger's concoction. "I was surprised at her interest but it came from her sister's addiction," she said. "And with Swagger out of the way, I won't have to ask the medical board to analyze the ingredients"

"Until Crane hooks up with another confidence man," Ambrose said. "I wouldn't put it past him."

"Well, I'm glad it's over and we know who killed Jenny and that it wasn't one of our people here. That bothered me more than anything."

"You solved it, Gracie." Smiling at her, Ambrose finished his oysters and pushed the plate from him.

She did the same and said happily, "The drive will soon reach Glens Falls, spring is on its way here, and the constable should be back as well."

Ambrose frowned.

"What is it?" Her words shouldn't have brought that reaction.

"I heard this when I was at the jail, Gracie."

"More?"

"I didn't want to spoil our dinner but you brought up the constable."

"Now what's he done, Ambrose?"

"Gone and died, I'm afraid."

"What?" She raised her napkin to her lips. She'd always detested the man for his interfering, gossipy ways, but never enough to wish him dead.

"How? How did he die?" She hoped by no one's violent hands. She'd had enough of murder.

"The stage from Utica overturned and he was thrown out. Hit his head on a boulder, they told me. Another stage carried him back home but word was sent to the county sheriff."

She remained silent, remembering her unhappiness with the man.

After a time he interrupted her thoughts. "They'll be needing a new constable for the town of Johnsburg, Gracie." He looked at her to see her reaction. She said nothing.

"I think it should be you," he said.

She raised shocked eyes to meet his and then laughed. Surely he was joking. But he appeared to be serious.

"You know that's impossible, Ambrose, even if you jest. The law doesn't even allow me to vote. How could I possibly become constable?"

"Yet you're the one people expect to solve things," he answered.

"Did they suggest anyone to you when you talked with the sheriff? Anyone we know?"

Ambrose looked embarrassed. "As a matter of fact, they did." He looked relieved when Annie appeared with their entree of pork medallions and set the platter down after removing their oyster plates. He looked as if he needed time to think about how to answer.

"Well," she pressed, "are you going to tell me?" Why was Ambrose acting so uncomfortably? And then she guessed and light laughter emerged.

"You! They suggested you as constable and you didn't want to tell me."

Ambrose's face colored. She wasn't sure she'd ever seen him like that.

"But that's wonderful, Ambrose! It makes sense. Your military background and all."

"I haven't been here that long, Gracie. I'm surprised anyone even thought of it."

"They thought of it because you brought in two prisoners involved in crime right here. That's why."

"Crimes you solved," he said.

"Well, if you are the constable, I can go on helping you solve them," she answered.

"There will be an election, you understand. Someone else might want the job."

"With all the friends you've made in this town, in this hamlet, you will certainly win the job if you want it," she assured him.

"I rather like the idea of floating your name, Gracie, to see if it would advance your cause for women's rights."

"Let's get some of those legal rights Susan Anthony is pressing for first, Ambrose. Then maybe if we achieve that we can think about women candidates all of us can vote for. In the meantime you have my vote."

Ambrose leaned toward her conspiratorially and whispered, "Thank you, Gracie, for that vote of confidence. I hate to remind you but you don't have one. One that will secure my election."

Their laughter caused Annie to look over at their table. They seemed to be enjoying themselves in spite of all the awful things that had happened. Annie knew there was no one smarter or kinder than Miss Wickham, and she would cross her heart and swear she would never say it out loud, but she did think it: Whatever was it in that skinny, unfashionable spinster that made Mr. Baldoon look at her like that?

HISTORICAL NOTES

New York's Hudson River—this body of water takes a 315 mile journey from the Adirondacks High Peaks to the Atlantic Ocean. At 4,322 feet above the sea level, the Hudson begins as a tiny stream flowing from a small pond known as Lake Tear of the Clouds. It eventually becomes a mile wide tidal river with depths well over 100 feet. All of the streams, lakes and ponds draining into the Hudson River are important parts of its watershed.

Logging Industry— Logging in the upper Hudson watershed had reached its peak in 1872 with a total of 213,800,000 board feet (from *Lumberjacks and Loggers in the* Adirondacks *1850-1950,* published by Blue Mt. Lake Museum).

The last Hudson River drive ended in the 1950's when the logs coming down to Glens Falls were used for pulp. Today's logs continue to travel south to Glens Falls on the back of huge trucks on the Northway's Interstate 87.

John E. Donahue—Jack Donahue 1865-1940 was in charge of the Hudson River drive from 1885 to 1939 and is the character that fictitious John Dillon is based on. He is the father of Milda Donahue Burns and Helen Donahue, two of his six children who aided my research. I used his true story of being paid at the end of a season in the woods with a pair of loggers' mittens and his father's advice to be "the one directing" in one of the chapters.

Godey's Lady's Book—with a circulation of 150,000 at the start of the Civil War, this was the most successful women's magazine in the United States. This monthly publication included fashions, etiquette, receipts, patterns, short stories and poetry, as well as health advice, helpful hints, and musical scores. Sarah Josepha Hale was the editor who urged President Lincoln to set aside a day for Thanksgiving.

Patented Medicine—Congress passed Patent legislation in 1793 to protect product ingredients. Not wanting to reveal ingredients of mainly alcohol and vegetable extracts, manufacturers In the 19th century instead sought patents on the shape of the bottle, promotional materials and label information. "Lydia Pinkham's Vegetable Compound" was the most successful patent medicine of the century, promoted in Boston newspapers in 1876 with her picture.

Mourning hair—The Swedes developed hair jewelry into a folk art in the late 16th century with mourning accessories from the hair of a deceased friend or loved one. Mourning in19[th] century United States was a respectful and fashionable practice even before the widow Queen Victoria issued a mandate that only mourning jewelry and hair jewelry would be worn at court. Mourning fashion and customs included hair jewelry in lockets, bracelets, brooches, and watch fobs among other items. Patterns for creating hair jewelry could be found in Godey's Lady's Book and popular pamphlets of the time.

In a previous incarnation, Rosemary Miner taught 11th grade American History. Her historical cozies, *Once Upon A Time To Die For* and *Lies and Logs To Die For*, are set in the Adirondack Mountains in the 1870's. Her novels bring to life the stories and history of the local people with the customs and commerce of the time. Rosemary is a member of Sisters in Crime, The Historical Novel Society and Mystery Writers of America.

9 781591 332558